The Book of Flying

Illustrated by the author

Riverhead Books
a member of Penguin Group (USA) Inc.
New York 2004

The Book of Flying

Keith Miller

In Chapter 6, page 139, Narya's line "How alien, alas, are the streets of the city of grief" is taken from Rainer Maria Rilke's tenth *Duino Elegy*, translated by Stephen Mitchell. The story of Narya's birth is adapted from Lafcadio Hearn's *Writings from Japan*, edited by Francis King.

This is a work of fiction. Names, characters, places, and incidents either are the product of the author's imagination or are used fictitiously, and any resemblance to actual persons, living or dead, business establishments, events, or locales is entirely coincidental.

Riverhead Books
a member of
Penguin Group (USA) Inc.
375 Hudson Street
New York, NY 10014

Library of Congress Cataloging-in-Publication Data

Miller, Keith, date.
The book of flying : a novel / Keith Miller.
p. cm.
ISBN 1-57322-249-6 (acid-free paper)
1. Librarians—Fiction. 2. Orphans—Fiction.
3. Adventure fiction. I. Title.
PS3613.I5396B66 2004   2003046913
813'.6—dc21

Printed in the United States of America
1   3   5   7   9   10   8   6   4   2

This book is printed on acid-free paper. ∞

Book design by Erin Benach

For Sofia

Acknowledgments

The author would like to thank Wendy Carlton
and Jimmy Vines for their assistance.

Contents

One

The Sad Poet and His Library

I am dreaming. I'm dreaming of a city, a white city in the sun by the sea, a city of bells and birdcages, boatswains and ballyhoo, where heart-faced wenches lean bare-breasted from balconies to dry their hair among geraniums and the air is salt and soft and in the harbor sailors swagger from ships that bear cargos of spices. In this city a thousand doves live in the hundred towers of a hundred bells and in the mornings when the bell ringers toll a summons to the sun the doves scatter like blown ash across the tile roofs and light under eaves whispering lulling words to sleepers, bidding them stay in bed a little longer. And on the silver sky other wings rise.

The city is filled with parks and bazaars. In the cool of the morning vendors cry their wares, pocket watches, pomegranates, parakeets, silks and cinnamon sticks, kittens and tea cozies, amber, sandalwood, baskets and blue glass beads. Magicians pull scarlet scarves and coins from ears, troubadours pull ballads from lyres and mandolins. In the shade of fig trees old men play checkers, casting winks at passing maidens, and old women on park benches giggle and gossip watching their grandchildren flounder in fountains.

The diners push back their chairs. They finish their luncheons with coffee and brandy and black cigarettes, and beyond their conversations seagulls keen and waves gnash at pilings.

In the hot afternoons the whole city sleeps, shuttered indoors in whitewashed rooms while chunks of light crawl slowly up walls like bright sluggish insects.

In the evenings the heart-faced girls dance on the sand to the music of lyres. They dance near fires and the young men watch the lick of the flames on their oiled arms. When the dancing subsides and the fires withdraw their yellow talons and crouch beneath ash peering out with red eyes, the youth quench their craving with whisky and watch wings wheel among the constellations.

For some of the people of the city are winged and when the sea shifts in the morning they pirouette on pinnacles, embrace the air and skim the waves calling to the dolphins and sailfish beneath them. Their wings are long, their eyes aflame and when they sing their speech is half the speech of birds. They fly at dawn and dusk and sometimes, if the moon is full, if the wind is right, they fly at night, slicing the sky to ribbons with the edges of their wings.

At city's edge, on the lower slopes of a hill, a small building of gray stone stands surmounted by dome and cupola, carven about with creatures, beings half human—half beast leaning from the walls as if striving for liberty. Beyond the great copper doors the floor is polished marble pieced in patterns and high on the walls and across the circular ceiling people are painted and some of them are winged. But most of the wall space is rosewood shelving and on the shelves are books, for this is a library. Among the stacked and voiceless words, in that scent of old leather and parched grass, a young librarian lives alone.

The books are ancient, gathered a century and more before his birth, and no one comes any longer to the library, only sometimes a grandmother might bring her grandchild to look at a volume of hand-tinted engravings, but they never ask to borrow. And when the librarian approaches bearing more books he thinks they might enjoy they glance at the covers politely and smile without meeting his eyes and walk back out into the sunlight. The librarian stands at the door watching, knowing they will not return.

His name is Pico. He is pale from days indoors, thin from forgetting to eat. He cares fastidiously for the library no one comes to, sweeping and mopping the floor, dusting the books with ostrich plumes, watering the irises that grow beside the door. He is vigilant against mice, silverfish, wary of fire. And he loves to read. He loves the whisper of the pages and the way his fingertips catch on rough paper, the pour of the words up from the leaves, through the soft light, into his eyes, the mute voice in his ears. He has read all the books, many several times, sitting at his massive mahogany desk in a corner of the room, the only sounds that of a bumblebee fumbling at the frescoes and the hiss of the turning pages.

In the evenings the librarian dons a blue velvet coat and a purple cravat and a black hat, the fashion of a prior generation, and with his pocketknife cuts an iris from the flower bed. Locking the library behind him he descends into the streets of the town and paces the cobblestones down to the sea, clutching the flower to his chest, smiling sadly at the children who shy away. Above the beach is a coral wall and he pulls a white handkerchief from a coat pocket and spreads it carefully upon the stone and sits there beside drying nets, watching the winged people as they circle and call above the salt water.

When they quit their cavorting and cant back across the beach returning to their towers he casts the iris into the swells and walks again through the town. He stops to buy bread, goat cheese, olives, pickled mushrooms and a bottle of milk and then returns to the library. He enters and climbs a circular staircase to the cupola, a little room open on all sides to breezes, though it has shutters against the rain. Seven black cats tumble from the windowsills and knock their skulls against his shins. He lights a candle and pours the milk into a bowl and they whine and rumble as they drink.

On the windowsill facing the sea are an embroidered cushion and a squat glass inkwell. The librarian sits cross-legged on the cushion nibbling at his supper and after a while fetches a leather-bound notebook and a green-and-gold fountain pen from beneath a mattress on the floor and fills the pen with purple ink and perched there above the city he writes poems by candlelight, or sometimes, if the moon is round, by that old light alone. He looks up often from the page, peering down over the thicket of towers where lamps are snuffed now and then like extinguished stars.

He has a stack of parchment, bought from a merchant who acquired it overseas, and sometimes he will take a sheet, rub it down with chalk and carefully copy onto it a poem from his notebook, twining fanciful creatures around the capitals, coloring them from a box of paints. When the paint is dry he rolls the parchment, ties it with yellow cord and over the knot drips a button of scarlet wax. Long after midnight he descends to the town, to a certain tower, which he climbs until he reaches a certain door. Beneath this door he slips the gift, then dashes back through the cobbled streets arriving breathless at the library. These nights he does not sleep and the mornings after these escapades does not open the brass-studded doors but sits on the windowsill in the cupola, not writing, not reading, oblivious to the cats whining on his lap, staring at the sea and the sky.

In the city the winged and the wingless mingle in marketplace and cafe, but they live apart, the winged in high towers among bells and doves, the others below, beside the streets, and they say it has always been so. Yet sometimes a winged child is born to parents wingless and is sent aloft and sometimes an earthbound child is born to flying parents and must go to live a life beneath the sky.

And so it was with Pico. His mother had wept when he slid from her body, a poppied runt, with no wet wings plastered to his shoulder blades. She suckled him but knew he could not stay in the sky-walled room atop the tower where his first steps might send him plummeting to the cobblestones. So she found an old librarian willing to take an apprentice, and the boy grew up in that book-walled house and learned to read before he could walk. The old man died in Pico's tenth year and the boy buried the body beside the door and planted irises on the grave, bulbs that bore dark blooms, faint tracings on their petals like the ghosts of words on charred paper.

The young librarian always went to the shore at dusk to watch the winged people on the wind, his mother among them. One evening in stormy weather a gust yanked a young girl into the surf where she floundered screaming, feathers waterlogged. Pico bounded into the water and pulled her to shore. He held her head while she gagged up brine and then her people dropped to the strand, wings drubbing the air, and they patted his skull and his mother kissed his cheek and they swept the girl away to a tower to recover.

Some weeks later as he read in the library he heard a flurry outside the door and going to the entrance saw a young girl, naked and winged, standing in the iris bed, and he remembered her face.

"You saved me from the sea," she said.

"They didn't tell me your name," he whispered. "I don't know your name."

"My name is Sisi. And you are Pico, your mother said."

"Do you like to read?"

She didn't know how to read but she perched on the desk, feet drawn up beneath her, and listened as he spoke from a book and when he was done she clapped her hands, then looked around.

"All these books are filled with stories?" she asked and he nodded.

"Then teach me," she cried. "Teach me to read."

And so over the next months she came to the library every morning and he taught her the letters and the words and gave her simple books gaudy with pictures that she took home to her tower. But more than reading alone she loved to hear him read aloud and soon he began as well to tell her tales received, he said, from an inner sky vaster than the one she traversed.

"Tell me a tale," she would beg. "Tell me, Pico." And they'd sit together on the steps of the library, by the bed of irises.

"Somewhere," he told her, "somewhere else lived a boy and a girl beside the sea and as they grew older they grew more transparent. At first blue blood vessels and then bones bloomed beneath the skin but soon they could see the shapes of the world behind their bodies, the shudder of leaves like shadows in the brain, a butterfly's flutter in the mutter of the heart, beetles in the coils of the bowels. They watched wine whirl down each other's throats and the sun rise up each other's spines, stepping vertically vertebra to vertebra. Soon the only substance they obtained was when their bodies overlapped and so they clasped each other, peering for the vestiges of eyes, teeth, ears, smears against the landscape. And one day they kissed and disappeared."

"You tell such beautiful stories." She would ruffle his hair. "How do you think of them?"

"At night, when you're flying, I'm dreaming."

"I have dreams too but I can't tell stories like you."

"You can fly."

"Yes. I can fly."

Though it was not uncommon for the winged and the unwinged to form friendships, the companionship of Pico and Sisi caused consternation when she began forsaking her flights at dusk for Pico's chatter. More often now she'd fly alone in the afternoons or late at night, listing lazily from wind to wind while Pico watched enraptured. They parted only to sleep.

The scandal erupted one day when her father spied them kissing in a borrowed sailboat. He had flown out to find her and when he spotted the two entwined in bilgewater near the reef he banged onto the wet planks and tipped Pico overboard to swim to shore.

After that they met in secret, though Sisi's tribe watched her so closely she could seldom sneak off. She poured her passion into flight and slowly the splendor of soaring bore away her desire for stories and so one evening in the shadows of the library Sisi told Pico that he could never comprehend her, that her whole life was flight while he was doomed to trudge the dust, his lust for sky unrequited.

"But the kisses," he said.

"They were only half kisses and this you know," she told him. "I could never wholly kiss a wingless boy. The taste of sky is absent from your tongue." And he felt that he knew this, that what he sought on her lips was what he lacked, and he beat his face with his fists and began to batter books about the room, barely hearing her whimper, "Now I'm going."

He sat by the sea and wept. He sat in the windows of his cupola. He sat at his desk and words became his world. He read and read, and the stories became his only delight. And he found one day among the volumes of the library a fat leather-bound book with gilt edges to its blank pages and he purchased a green-and-gold fountain pen from a purveyor of curiosities and he made his own purple ink from oak galls and oyster shells and with these tools began to quarry poems, the pages filling slowly as stone dust fills a valley floor.

And sometimes he'd carry a poem in secret to a girl who lived atop a tower and whether she read it or burned it he did not know, for she never replied.

One morning as he trod the spiral staircase down to the library he saw that a mushroom big as a baby's head had, with uncanny vegetable strength, butted up a marble slab in the center of the room. He plucked the mushroom and carried it to his desk and then returned to replace the square of stone. But as he bent over the hollow where it had lain he glimpsed a pale curve that he took for shell or root, but when he'd brushed the dirt away saw was the flank of a porcelain jar. He pulled the jar free and placed it on the desk beside the mushroom, thumbing crumbs of soil from its lip. He withdrew the clay stopper, reached a wrist into the mouth and lifted forth an ebony box. Trembling, he prized away the lid and found, beneath old oiled silk, a single sheet of folded paper that splintered along the creases as he splayed it. In the opal morning light Pico bent to read:

I am old and the city burns below me as I write. All the towers are flame and the breakers blush. In my room above the city, sitting above books, I scrawl a missive to you who will follow, for though the library will burn, yet it has burned before and been rebuilt, books brought from islands beyond the horizon to fill the shelves. The line of librarians will remain, of this I am certain.

The winged have flown, or died as they fled the torched towers, arrows in their breasts, and in the streets the fools, soused on destruction, perpetuate their folly. The whole city by dawn will be cinders. My prentice, a wanton lad swayed ever by the masses, claimed before he set off to join the mayhem that a winged boy had loved an earthbound girl and, forbidden by his parents to have her, had drowned himself in the sea. The books of this library are filled with such tales and, whether true or not, they kindle the flames that now flit on this paper. When will the wingless learn that the wings are within them, that their very seed feeds their envy, that from their own loins the feathered lineage will resurge?

From readings of the books of this library and from the tales of my predecessor, I have surmised that the fabled town of Paunpuam, the morning town, lies not over the sea, as some say, but eastward beyond the forest. Counter to contemporary insistence, the older volumes claim that the forest indeed has an end and is traversable to one with fortitude and good fortune, though its trials are manifold, fearsome. And beyond the forest are other obstacles, named and unnamed, before one reaches the ruined town where one may read the Book of Flying and gain wings.

I will arise now and cache this letter where flames may not find it, though you will, you have, how many years hence. I will shoulder my knapsack and set off toward a figment and will find it or perish in the undertaking. I see them swarming from the city now. Some have strapped severed wings to their forearms and flap them insanely and all have bloody feathers in their hair. I must make haste. I go to seek my wings.

That evening Pico built a fire on the hillside, well away from the library walls for like all booklovers he feared inferno. He roasted the mushroom spitted on a green stick and pondered the letter it had revealed. The fable of the morning town was known to him, from snippets in books, from street chatter, whispers of a faraway place, a school for flying where the flightless might gain their wings. But though that town had inhabited his poems, his dreams, until this day he'd guessed it a forlorn gesture, desire manifest in story. But this predecessor who'd paced the same stone floor, who'd curled likewise in the windowsills of the cupola, had worn this story like a coat, had pulled it over his feet like boots and set off into the forest while his books burned behind him.

He broke a morsel off the mushroom and placed it on his tongue. The flames at his heels suddenly swelled into the world all around and he gazed through a gauze of heat across a desert amid whose sands stood a ruined town and into the tawny air from cropped towers and toppled arches leaped, like lifting leaves in a dust devil, winged people rising to the sun. Over the morning town of Paunpuam the winged ones circled, and then the night once more drew close and Pico plucked the hissing mushroom from the coals.

The following morning he rose early, pocketed a few gold coins and walked down to the bazaar. Among the barking hawkers he wandered, pausing to peruse the knicknacks, bric-a-brac, trinkets trundled here from ports beyond the world's edge. He pondered maps of strange lands, curious cloths, queer caged birds, and the merchants cajoled him to part with his coins.

He bought a compass cased in brass, a supply of candles, a small tin pot with a wire handle, a corked water bottle, a ball of twine, a gray woolen blanket, an oilcloth groundsheet and a canvas knapsack. He searched the tailors' stalls till he found shirts and trousers of tough stuff. From a cobbler he purchased a pair of sturdy black boots.

"Voyaging, are you?" the cobbler cocked an eye to the pack, and Pico smiled and replied, "I leave on the morrow to seek my wings," at which the cobbler grinned uncertainly and bent to his last.

With the remaining money Pico bought a jar of pickled herrings, a loaf of crusty bread, several smoked sausages and a round of hard cheese from the food stalls and returned to the library with his provisions.

At dusk he plucked a last iris and descended a last time to the shore, to the coral wall to watch the winged people. He thought Sisi had never flown more prettily, her wings bright as mica on the granite sky. Pico did not know whether she saw him that evening, for she never looked down, and when the winged people swept overhead to their houses, arabesqueing, he cast his iris into the surf in a gesture sorrowful but also reverential for he had witnessed his heart's desire fired by the art she revered, reveling, revelatory, glorified.

.   .   .

So the poet, in baggy trousers tucked into red and white striped kneesocks, in new boots and a blue work shirt, an old-fashioned hat on his head, exited the library at sunrise. The books were all in order and he had swept and mopped the floor and carefully he locked the door and placed the key under the mat, though he left the cupola shutters ajar for the cats to get at their last saucer of milk. He swung his knapsack to his shoulders, staggered lightly, swiveled welling eyes to the town where bells binged and bonged and wings big and small sprawled from towers to greet the sun, and then he turned to the forest.

At first it seemed he could make no headway. Thorns snagged his pack, snatched his hat, the creepers coiled about his thighs, and he could barely see. But slowly his eyes focused to the shadows and his heart quit its capering. He cut a staff from a bush and with its aid began to struggle through the wood. After what seemed like hours he straightened and looked behind him and almost wept to still see slivers of sky. His yearning for home was suddenly so strong he nearly turned, but then remembered the vision in the fire, the wings above the desert, and he set his fingers to the next vine and the next and when later he looked around again found himself in unsundered darkness.

In late afternoon his knees buckled and he slumped against a tree root and lay looking up to the sieved sky. After a while he pulled free of his pack and rummaging in it found the water bottle and the loaf of bread and he ate and drank. Scratches hatched his hands, his clothes were rent, hat battered. In the absence of his clamber the sounds of the forest surfaced to his ears, far coughing, close rustling, a gibber, a twitter, a twig crack. Lovebirds pulsed like painted hearts in the twilight, a snake swept past, tongue flickering from an arrowhead.

As the light failed he cleared a space in the undergrowth, gathered sticks and lit a fire. He filled his tin pot with water, hung it from a stake above the blaze and spread his groundsheet and blanket nearby. The root made a shelf to hold his ink bottle and pen, his leather-bound notebook and three favorite books borrowed from the library, books sturdy under the weight of rereading. A book of poems, a dense novel, a volume of queer stories. When the water boiled he added chamomile flowers from a cotton pouch and poured the tea into a cup. In the round room his fire made, the poet read and wrote and wept a little, sipping chamomile tea, looking up now and then to stir the coals, lay on twigs. Early he slipped into uncertain slumber, his pack his pillow, and several times during the night sat up sputtering, fingers staving off figments, leopards, adders, men, then lay back, hand to throat, trying to quell his dashing heart.

In the morning the forest seemed friendlier, the bird stammer merry. He blew the embers into flame, brewed himself a mouthful of coffee, toasted a slice of bread, then packed his possessions, peered at the compass and pursued his path eastward.

Two

The Robber Queen

Three days he floundered forward. He found plenty of brooks to replenish his water supply but on the morning of the third day devoured the butt end of his last sausage and though he scoured the undergrowth for mushrooms or familiar fruits his supper was chamomile tea. The next day he found some nuts but nothing else. Though he grew more adept at squirming through the undergrowth he made paltry progress, so he was elated when, on the third day, he struck a path leading southeast. The trail was scant, a meandering sliver of easier walking, but barrier free. The prints of boar and gazelle showed on bare earth but he was surprised to see as well the traces of bootheels, for he'd not thought humans dwelt this deep. Now he tossed aside his stick and strode swiftly, delighted to swing his arms, straighten his spine.

Late in the afternoon from an eye's edge he glimpsed a spangle of gold and a splash of sun on steel but before he could squeal his feet were swiped from under him and he lay with his face against the leaves while his pack was hauled from his shoulders. A boot tipped him onto his back and he looked up into three grizzled faces and the cold snouts of three knives cocked at his neck.

"Your money or your life," a bandit snarled.

"I haven't any money," Pico faltered, "so I suppose you'll have to take my life."

"Arr," said another, "we'll see what Adevi says about that." He yanked Pico upright, bound his hands and they set off along the trail.

They walked for an hour while the light failed, the bandits prodding him in the spine if they felt he wasn't walking fast enough and at last, through the trees ahead, he saw the twinkle of firelight.

In the sloe-eyed night the bonfire of the robber camp was ringed by tambourines rung by twirling girls wearing only patched skirts and bangles, pearl-decked anklets and great gold earrings. The men sat on logs they sometimes slapped and sometimes they clapped intricate counterpoint to the patter of slim feet. The robbers were stubble-jawed, their eyes blade-sharp, blood-dark, fingers nimble as lizards. They wore open shirts, chains on chests, embroidered vests, hoops in lobes, colored kerchiefs, brass-buckled boots. Incessantly they honed knives to edges which might slice flesh as easily as entering water, incessantly they smoked black tobacco turned into licked papers, the cigarettes lit from firebrands.

Night is the thief's domain and if he's not stealing he'll pass the hours under moonbeam, starshine, singing and boasting. Daytime's for dreams, lovemaking among shadows, but night's the country of the robber's heart and he'll always stay awake till dawn.

Pico, trussed, lay on the outskirts of the firelight entranced by the melodies, the twinkle of ankles beneath gusting skirts, the swing of honey-filled breasts. The fire pooled and siphoned color, the color of cloth like the color of jewels, bloodstone, black opal, lapis lazuli, emerald, a necklace about a hot throat. The flames snapped their fingers at the stars. Then amid the dancing girls a robber rose like an uncoiling cobra, and Pico saw when the fire flapped at the robber's face it was a woman, her eyes green as brass. She called a tall bandit to her and the girls subsided as, pelvis vised to pelvis, the two strutted round the circle rocking like clock weights. The man dipped her till her hair scooted over the flames, and she laughed, a noise like a landslide.

Her name was Adevi and she was the robber queen, pretty as a leopard, with a voice like rocks shaken in a cauldron, a tongue swift as a whip, haunches hard as though carven. All night the thieves told tales of their exploits and she was at the center of most, her deeds more daring than any, her audacity outlandish. Above the brand on her forearm was a constellation of scars, one for every death at her hands, some of them recent. She could touch a scar and tell a tale of murder. Pico heard that night stories to rival any recounted in the books of the library, fifty locks picked to snatch a stick of silver, tower walls scaled towing laden swags, families murdered in their sleep, half a town set alight to reach a cache of rubies. He was appalled, enthralled.

After midnight she came to him, sliced away his bonds and straddled a log beside him, making a cigarette while he rubbed his wrists.

"Have a smoke," she said and poked the cigarette between his lips, rolling another one-handed while fetching a brand from the fire. He didn't smoke but felt it polite to partake under the circumstances so he leaned forward to receive her flame. The first suck caused such a chaos of coughing she had to whack his back while the collected company howled.

"And I'll bet you're a virgin too," she said as he sat back, eyes awash. He nodded. "But I've kissed a girl before," he said, then clutched his palms to his cheeks which seemed suddenly feverish.

"Been awhile since you talked with a woman?" she asked and he nodded again but still could not meet her eyes.

She undid the drawstring of his knapsack and emptied it onto the ground, rifling through the heap while the robbers looked on. She pocketed the compass and tried on the blue velvet coat but found it too narrow in the shoulders. The books she splayed, peered at bemusedly, then made to cast them into the fire but at this Pico wailed.

"Not my books," he cried. "Take my other possessions, anything you like, but not my books, oh please spare my books."

"What use are they?" Adevi asked, flipping through his notebook.

"They tell stories if you know how to read. They are worlds, filled with all manner of people and places. Here," and he stretched to take one but she lifted it out of reach.

"Perhaps they have some value, Adevi," an onlooker suggested and she shrugged and swept the volumes aside.

"So, intruder," she turned to him. "Are you a lost hunter or a spy from another band? Speak carefully now. The queen of lies has an ear for the truth."

He sat straight-backed and looked around the ring of faces. "My name is Pico," he said, "and I come from the city by the sea. I am a librarian by trade, a caretaker of books, those objects you so nearly tossed into the fire. I doubt they would fetch anything in the market as I was the city's sole collector of such oddities. My tale is this. As a boy I loved a winged girl but due to certain conventions we were forced apart. My parents too were winged, but by a fluke of birth I am wingless, my desire denied me by the fickle fingers of fate, and the only hope I have of holding my love again is to acquire wings. So when one day a mushroom revealed a letter from a long-dead librarian claiming that the morning town, legendarily the site of the school for flying, lies not overseas but eastward, beyond the forest's far side, I packed my knapsack and set out to seek my wings or die in the attempt. Three days I struggled forward till yesterday when I found the path that led me into the ambush of your men."

"It's clear you're telling the truth," Adevi said, "but you're a simpleton if you think there's an end to the forest or, if there was one, that you could reach it. Men," she swiveled to the robbers, "which of you would be willing to accompany this lad farther east?"

At that the throng muttered and shuffled.

"Not so foolhardy," one mumbled.

"I'll meet any man hand to hand," another said, "but there are unnatural beings in the woods. It's not fair fighting something more than human, or less. We keep to our side, they keep to theirs, that's what I say." And the other robbers growled agreement.

"You'll meet any man, you say," Adevi called to him, "but are you a match for a woman?" and the robber scowled and blushed, twisting a stick in the fire while the band jeered, though all in fact feared their captain.

"A cowardly lot, admittedly," Adevi turned back to Pico, "but their fear might be rooted in something real."

"I am on a quest," he told her. "I must find my wings or perish in the undertaking."

"You're not afraid of monsters?" and there was an avidness in her glance.

"Of course I'm afraid but this is my path."

"Well this is all chatter anyway," she said briskly, snapping her cigarette into the fire. "Your journey ends here. Will you join my robber band? Will you let us brand your forearm?" She pushed up a sleeve and displayed the symbol, a sickle moon. "Will you join our midnight adventures? The robber's life is rough but the prizes are the racing heart, the moonlit dancing, the hot spurt of blood on the hand and of course the gold, the gold." And she dipped a wrist into a pocket and tipped a rivulet of coins at Pico's feet.

"Do I have another option?" he asked.

"Cold steel in your neck," she replied and began to pare her fingernails with the tip of her falchion.

"Well I guess I'll become a thief, then," said Pico unhappily, "though I don't think I'll be much good. I'm a pacifist, you see." But Adevi paid him no heed. "Men, gather round," she shouted. "Welcome your new comrade."

The robbers stood in a ring about Pico and bade him place his left palm on the outthrust points of their knives and recite the following oath: "By the dirk's edge and the dark side of the moon, by the glitter of gold and the hot hammer of blood I swear to be true to the robber tribe and to Adevi, my chieftain." Then all the bandits slashed their palms and Adevi seized Pico's fingers and gashed his hand and he clasped each of the robbers' fists in turn, passing crimson handshakes around the circle.

"We must have a toast," Adevi yelled. "What will you drink, lad?"

"I believe I'll have a glass of white wine," Pico said and the company guffawed. Adevi scowled. "There's whisky or rum, what'll it be?"

"Rum, then," he mumbled.

They uncorked squat square bottles and someone gave Pico a cut-crystal tumbler and tipped a portion of viscous liquid into it. He dipped a cautious tongue then sipped slowly, the alcohol lava in his belly. Adevi cast him a green wink and he lifted the glass with a tentative grin. His legs soon swayed under him and he had difficulty bringing the brim to his lips but was glad for the daze when a smirking bandit approached with a cherry-bright brand, called others to hold Pico down and pressed the iron into his flesh, the grilled odor gagging him, the delayed pain insane.

The robbers' tents tugged guylines in the sway of breezes, the fire pit faced by their triangular doorways, and robbers slept half out of these shelters, still clutching whisky bottles as though fearful a companion might nab them as they napped. Circling the camp as some gesture toward adornment, human skulls were set upturned like cups on logs and snapdragons spilled from their soil-filled brainpans, sprouting out eye sockets, nodding on loose molars. All around the camp were scattered signs of an incongruous decadence, plush armchairs, brass lamps, fancy end tables, paintings in gilt frames, the rotting flotsam of robberies. The bandits ate meat from spits of green wood, together with fine caviar and aged cheeses, off fancy china with their fingers, and they gulped their rum from golden goblets. Their attire was sumptuous, a hodgepodge of articles lifted from the wardrobes of the city, though linen trousers were grease-spotted, silk shirts blood-spattered. They pampered only their knives.

Adevi presided from a green canvas pavilion open to the rest of the camp and there she rutted in the day with her companion of the moment, on a soiled divan, two daggers sunk in the cladding of its arm, her shouts barging through the wood. After these encounters she rose naked, hair like the brush of an old broom, and straddled the embers to piss, steam hissing between her thighs, and Pico did not know where to look.

His second day in the camp as he returned from filling his plate at the fire a robber knocked him to the ground and when he struggled up knocked him down again. He looked up into a bearded leer. "Can't keep your balance, pretty boy?" The bandit lifted Pico by the hair and seized him between the legs. "Come on, pretty boy, you're a robber now, let's see you scrap." Pico slapped at the bandit's face and with more luck than aim caught the base of the crooked nose with the heel of his hand. The robber released him with a grunt and Pico fell to the ground and began to cry. Through tears he glimpsed a steel-tipped boot drawn back and cringed but the blow never arrived. As he cowered he heard a gasp and a gurgle and the ground shivered. He looked up to see the bandit jerking beside him and wondered if it was some sort of fit and then saw a knife handle like a sudden cancer sprouted from the man's neck. His eyes were fixed on Pico's face with a look of terror such as the poet had never seen and then white washed across them and blood spilled from his lips. Adevi strode up and bent to retrieve her knife, wiping it on the dead man's trousers. She looked around at the robbers, some of whom had stopped eating to view the entertainment.

"You leave the librarian alone," she told them.

"But he's a liability, Adevi," one whined. "He hasn't got the guts for this life, let us practice our knife throwing on him."

"Would you go farther east with him?" Adevi asked. At that the robbers bent grumbling to their plates.

The arts of thievery are as old as the arts on which thieves thrive. Pico was given an ebony-handled dagger in a leather scabbard that he practiced tossing into a tree trunk, loving the hurtling steel star, the bump if it bedded in the wood, which it seldom did. He was made to mount tall trees, first as best he could, then laden with rock-filled sacks, and his palms blistered, suppurated and healed hard as the bark they clutched. He practiced picking a selection of locks, prying with a bent wire till the tumblers clicked and the tongue snapped back. And he acquired some of the robbers' argot.

In late afternoons he knife-fought in slow motion with Adevi, learning the feints and counters, when to slash, when to stab, learning to keep his feet flickering, torso angled away from the other's thrusts. She was so beautiful, sliding in and out of the shadows, that sometimes he felt they were dancing, that the banging of blades was part of some rehearsed ritual, and then he did well in matching her offense.

But if he thought about the purpose of the metal he wielded he slipped up and Adevi, an impatient instructor, flipped and pinned him, dagger point dimpling his neck.

He joined the fireside circle in the evenings, clapped in time to the tunes, and the dancing girls gathered round him. They braided his hair, pierced his ears and swayed him to allow a robber to tattoo his right arm, though he refused the scorpion the rogue wished to engrave and with mirror and eyeliner sketched onto his skinny bicep an iris.

The girls taught him to drink liquor and roll cigarettes, and over time he learned to lean into the ease of the nicotine, the heat of the alcohol, and came to look forward to the nights by the fire, his mind floating in the bowl of his skull.

"Why are you sad?" the girls asked and he told them of Sisi's oval lips, the shiver of her feathers against the sky, how her laughter fell to him like the promise of rain, and they sighed. He asked them how they came to this rowdy corner of the woods and they related stories of groping fathers or vindictive stepmothers, of unforeseen pregnancies or boredom with the pallid men of the city. Their hands were always on him as he listened, on his thin arms, stroking his pale cheeks, but he responded to their attentions so gravely the robbers had no cause for jealousy and in the days, when the camp quieted, when the girls coupled with the thieves, he retired alone to a cleared space. For though he could sleep in a tent if he wished, if the sky was dry he took the blanket allotted him and napped in the dappled dusk beneath the trees but not too far from the camp for the sentry on duty would harrumph and look up from honing his dirk if he strayed more than a stone's throw from the fire pit.

One moonless night, on a secret trail, Adevi led Pico back to the city by the sea and he chuckled to think he could have saved three days' struggle had he hit on this path from the first. They arrived above the city as the bells pealed at dawn and the winged people scattered from their towers and Pico thrilled to see again the wings above the sea. He looked as well at his little library on the slopes of the hill but felt no compulsion to return. It was no longer his home.

That day they slept at forest's edge and the next night descended to the streets he'd quit it seemed a year gone by and he paced the cobbles like one in a dream. Queer, he mused, that I must return to the place where I began my journey in order to continue it. But then perhaps not so strange after all for such is often the way with poems.

Bat shriek and starshine their only companions, Adevi and apprentice scaled walls and meandered above mazed alleys searching houses that concealed treasure. Pico was a mite, a bit of blown fluff aflit on a rooftop, up so high he wanted to sing, to call to the reeling night owls in the streets below, to scream a poem. Windowsill to doorframe to gable the thieves leaped, tripped across tiles and saw their shadows misshapen by swags framed on walls by starlight like the apparitions of lonely hunchbacks releasing frustrations in rooftop tantrums.

Adevi sent the thin-shouldered poet through a slit window and he tiptoed among the sighs of sleepers, dreamers surprisingly vocal, the air filled with unconscious conversation, to unbolt the door for his chief. Adevi took a candle from her bag and by that leaf of light they searched for gold. They upended inlaid boxes, probing beneath piled dresses, prying at loose bricks, hoping for the blond shimmer of the metal that stirred the blood. They ladled jewelry into bags, cushioned the clink with folded cloth, then wandered through rooms burdening themselves with loose jade, ivory statuettes, silver spoons, silk. In a cot a child clutched a porcelain-faced doll and this Adevi tweaked from tiny fingers and tossed to Pico. The child sighed and shifted on its sheets. Pico wondered what it would have been to be born in such a house with a mother to place a doll on your chest and tuck you in with a surfeit of kisses and arms to hold you if the wind at your window wailed too shrilly. The child fondled the air and when Adevi left the room he snuggled the doll back into its hug.

Then Adevi led him out over the rooftops to a great house above the harbor. Deftly she opened an upper window, a twitch of her knife lifting the latch. He followed her downstairs to a big room completely bare of furniture and watched bewildered while she locked the door and drew the curtains. Then she lit her candle and he saw the walls were paneled in paintings. Slowly they moved around the room, Adevi lifting her flame to each canvas in turn, her eyes on Pico's face, and he gasped and sighed, because the paintings were beautiful and strange, filled with winged fish and bird-headed men, trees with hands on the ends of their branches and girls with the legs of gazelles, all exquisitely detailed, the colors sumptuous, the faces of the creatures sad.

"So beautiful," Pico mumbled. He thought Adevi meant to steal one of these paintings but when she was sure he had seen all to his satisfaction she snuffed the light and opened the shutters and they exited through the upper window, which she closed behind her. Then they snuck along alleys avoiding lit bars and bantering drunks back to the forest's edge where Pico lit a fire while Adevi laid out their loot.

Among the items he'd lifted were a dusty bottle of wine, a loaf of bread and a wedge of cheese and he cut sandwiches for Adevi and himself and uncorked the wine and they sat with their backs to trees looking down the long slope to the shore where fires mocked the tide. The wine was good and Pico refilled Adevi's cup and then his own and they rolled cigarettes and sat sipping and smoking. He remembered an old poem:

"At journey's end, at evening,
arriving in a remote town,
I walk through deserted streets
to a certain house, knock upon a certain door,
and only as it opens do I see
I stand on my own doorstep
and beyond the threshold a road descends
anew through a landscape I left
so long ago."

The blush of Adevi's cigarette swelled her face from the shadows. "Once I would have killed you for that verse," she said.

"Don't you like poetry?" Pico asked, dismayed. "It's a fragment I wrote awhile ago, it seemed to match my mood tonight," but she was not looking at him.

"What brings a girl to the robber tribe?" she said. "What would cause a maiden to leave a city where she can dance all night by the sea, take coffee and pastries in cafes as bells ring at dawn, barter in bazaars for any trinket she can conceive of, where enough tales arrive from the ocean's six edges to keep lifetimes of listeners amused. Poverty, you might guess, but I was born in that last house, the great house by the docks. My parents were performers who earned their gold playing for the elite and our house was always filled with actors and musicians. What child growing up in that clamor of creation would not want to be an artist as well and such was my wish but it was not fated. All the talent went to my brother, younger by two years. He doodled in the dirt, in the food in his dish, and his gift was cherished, coddled like a living thing. He was skinny as you, librarian, with the same pale cheeks, always sneezing into silk handkerchiefs, often propped on pillows in a four-poster bed, doted on by doctors. My parents imported the finest paper and paints, stretched canvases that he filled with the fabulous figments of his fantasies. At fifteen he couldn't paint fast enough to supply the demand for his work and visitors arrived from afar to pay him homage, making obeisance as they would to a young prince. Yet it never seemed to affect him, all this praise, and his only wish was to retreat to his room, to the recesses of his imagination, and turn those inner worlds into images.

"But siblings are rivals whether they know it or not. In me grew such horror at my lack of talent that I knew one of us would have to die in order that the other could simply live. One afternoon I went into his room and the painting he labored over was so beautiful that emotion welled up inside me and I snatched the palette knife from his hand and slashed his throat. It felt so good. His blood colored the blank spaces in the canvas, a fulfilment. Yes, I killed my brother, of all deeds the most abhorrent, to save myself I killed him and then, though my parents might have thought the murder the act of an intruder, I had to leave the city altogether. I found my way to the bandits in the forest where I discovered I had a gift after all, a knack for killing.

"And so you see, librarian, I once would have stabbed you over a poem, for the revelation of another's talent always reminds me of my own barrenness, but in recent years I have begun to encourage the singing and dancing in the evenings, in the robber camp where I am queen. What else can I do, what else can I do?"

"Here," said Pico, "drink some more wine. Hold your cup steady. Let me roll you another cigarette."

Another night as they plundered the city Pico realized he was beneath the tower where Sisi lived and he asked Adevi to wait.

"But that's a house of winged people," Adevi said. "They own no gold."

"It's a different treasure I'm looking for," he replied and spiraled up the stairs and at the top picked a lock and entered a room of winds, bells bulbous above, a room bare save for a few teak chests. The winged people were asleep at the edges of the balustradeless balconies, crouched like great eagles, wings over their heads like feathered counterpanes.

Sisi was perched at the room's very lip, facing the waves, and he realized with a shock she was awake, no wing bent over her face, but the sea below was so loud she hadn't heard him. For a heady second he thought he'd walk over, talk to her, then shook his head at his folly. Reaching into his sack he silently retrieved a golden chain stolen earlier that night and draped it across the doorknob. He looked once again at Sisi, then closed the door and descended to Adevi.

On the peak of a rooftop they sat awhile in the domain of owls, cowled by stars, above the sea.

"Look there, at that coral wall the waves smash on," Pico said. "That's where I once sat watching the girl I love on the wind. Have you ever been in love, Adevi?"

"I've been with a hundred men and I've found that the less love enters in the better time I have in bed."

"Why so many? Wouldn't one be enough?"

"I have yet to meet a man who can quench my thirst. I'm looking for a man as strong as I am, stronger than meat, than liquor, a man brave as a frightened mother, with a heart hard as a tooth. The hearts of men are too easily stolen, they are not vigilant in guarding the gates of their ribs and my thieving fingers can always reach beneath the sternum and snatch it."

"What do you do with their hearts?"

"I eat them."

"Perhaps I'd be better off without a heart," Pico pondered, melancholy. "Without a heart I wouldn't have the desire to reach the morning town."

Adevi rolled a cigarette. "Tell me about this morning town."

"Paunpuam. I'd heard of the place as a child and always thought it was in the country of dreams. But now I believe the morning town exists in this world and one may walk there. From the books of the library and from a vision vouchsafed me before I undertook this journey I know it lies in a desert, tumbledown, the stones of its walls crumbling to sand. Among the ruins stands a tower greater than the others, rows of arched casements gazing across the dunes, and in that tower is kept the Book of Flying. Those who reach the town and enter the tower may read the book and learn to fly, may gain their wings. Over the morning town the winged ones rise, they rise on golden wings to the sun."

"Fool," she said, leaning back on the tiles. "You're living in your dreams. This is the world, this breeze on your face, this hot smoke in your lungs, this gold you can dent with your teeth. Learn to enjoy it or you'll never be happy."

"Happiness," sighed Pico, looking out at the first brown strands of dawn on the distant breakers. "Are you happy, Adevi?"

"I'm happy when I'm thieving."

"What about when you're alone at night. Are you happy then?"

"I'm never alone at night."

One afternoon she came to him, boisterous as always. "Up, poet, we're off to burgle," she shouted and he fetched his black sack and followed her along the path toward the city. After a few minutes she cut left into the woods and he opened his mouth but she placed a palm on his lips, whispering, "Follow."

Within dense undergrowth she uncovered a tarp and peeled it back.

"My knapsack!" Pico bent to undo the drawstring. He took his books in his hands, caressed them as he might a lover's skin, then looked up at Adevi. "Oh thank you, thank you." He stood and kissed her cheek. She swatted him away.

"Pick up your pack and follow me."

She hefted a pack of her own, concealed their swags and the tarp beneath bushes, then led him through the forest east and south, curling back in a long loop past the camp. He marveled at her movement, silent and lissome as an antelope's, while he struggled behind her. After an hour she straightened and walked less carefully and he caught up.

"Where are we going, Adevi?" he asked.

"We're running away," she grinned. "I've always wanted to explore the deep forest but none of those cowards would ever come with me, their mothers' stories too potent for them. It's no fun adventuring alone, but when you arrived with your hankering for the east I knew I'd found a companion."

"So you'll come with me to the morning town?" Pico cried.

"As far as I'm concerned the morning town's moonshine, but I'm not one to pass up an adventure and you'd never survive alone."

"Oh Adevi, how can I thank you?"

"Come on."

Led by a dream she doesn't believe in the robber queen guides the poet through the dark ways, through a domain which seems her own, she wafts among the trees like a breeze, and though the weeks of thievery have lightened Pico's step he feels stone-footed in her wake.

On the third evening of their travels Adevi stood across the fire from Pico and to the music of a nearby nightingale and the percussion of her snapping fingers began to dance. He watched through the window of heat that spindled and heightened her motions as she plucked the clothing from her body, the head scarf, vest, white shirt, skirt, all flung to catch on thorns until she churned like a raw demon aflame and he sat transfixed by the stare of her violet-eyed breasts. Then she came to him and held him down and he looked at her and said "Adevi—" as if he'd forgotten something but she covered his mouth with her hand.

Later he wept so violently she thought it was a fit but when she tried to touch him again he shuddered as though her fingers burned.

"So you're a virgin," she said, rolling a cigarette. "We all were once. You'll learn."

"You don't understand. I've betrayed her."

"Your winged girl?"

He nodded.

"Hasn't she been with other boys?"

He nodded.

"Then you're betraying only your own imagination."

"That's it precisely," Pico cried. "I've betrayed my imagination."

"Lie down."

But he made her promise that she would not try to touch him again and that night he lay awake, unable to read or write, the memory of the deed a needle in his heart. In the morning he couldn't eat and Adevi squatted before him.

"Look, poet, love is never what we think it will be. Love is like a boy trying to rescue a drowned girl from the sea and falling in himself."

"Yes, but what a beautiful death. Oh I wish I had drowned, I wish I had drowned."

"Love is two blind people sword-fighting, love is a queen on a desert island, love is self-immolation, love is running scared in the dark, love is two people each of whose saliva is poison for the other, love is an empty house, a sunken boat, a crippled dancer."

"Love is the memory of the scent of the breath of a sleeping girl," whispered Pico.

"Climb down out of your brain, poet. You're tangled in the cobwebs of your dreams. Welcome to the land of your body, with all its guilt, all its ecstasy."

But he would not look at her.

The sap rose in him again however, as it always does, drowning the memory of his shame, sending the tendrils of desire from his groin to his skull. So two days later he crept past the warm ashes of the fire long after midnight and crawled into the tides of her breathing and said, "Teach me."

For a week they only left camp to shoot game, for they were always starving. They did not have to go far, for the animals gathered round at evening to see this new beast of the forest, four-legged, two-headed, shouting.

"Don't think, don't think," Adevi gasped each night, each morning, and he entered her again and again as if he might fill the hollow space beneath his breastbone.

"It's like eating," he told her.

"It's like murder," she said and, shuddering, he kissed the glyphs of fifty deaths on her forearm. Those fingers which had cupped blood, stopped breath, now clutched his shoulder blades.

"What's it like to kill?" he asked.

"The pleasure is hidden. Like all the sweetest pleasures the first taste is bitter. The red grin beneath my brother's chin still curves beneath my eyelids, and unlike the nights of men in bed each murder since stays quite alone in my mind's eye, I can live each thrust again and again if I wish. It's the ultimate theft, the stealing of another's heartbeat."

"What about the dead? Where do they go?"

"No one has ever come back from that black doorway to say. It's the one true adventure, unknown, unknowable."

"You crave it?"

"I'm not afraid of it. That's why I don't lose my fights."

"I have wanted death as well, wanted it as badly as I've wanted a woman, to embrace it, to kiss those lavender lips, though I did not seek adventure but escape."

"There is no escape, poet. There's only the unwinding road. You follow the road or it follows you."

"I am trying. I'm trying to follow that road, to reach the morning town."

"You're living in your dreams."

"Yes, dreams are the seam I mine, the soil I till, the timber I fell. I am a carpenter, sawing, planing, hammering my dreams, jointing them into structures sturdy enough to bear the weight of a body, the weight of flesh. I have my tools, my notebook, my fountain pen."

"My tools are my knife, my hands."

"Your tongue, your breasts . . .

"The thief entered after midnight,
laid me down
with a blow to the skull,
bound my hands
and set a knife to my heart,
demanding my money.

"So I opened my lips,
licked away her clothes,
lifted my hips to hers
and poured my gold
into her satin purse."

The meeting between a sad poet and a thief could never be anything but forlorn. As the edges of the novelty were chamfered away Pico realized that his ache was a wound, always he tasted blood and knew it was his own.

"You have given me something," he told her. "But you've taken something away. In its place a new thing has grown and I must be alone to discover what it may be."

She had tried to take his heart but had only stolen his innocence. And what can a thief leave behind but the awareness of loss? So Pico in a progress through the unknown territory of the forest finally found words to write a sonnet to his distant winged girl and Adevi could only sit and watch. Her eyes, which had never lost their appetite, all over his body, her stare, which had never failed to cow men, bring them trembling to her side, now glancing unavailing off the intent poet.

In the days sometimes she drew her knife and came at him, forcing him to defend himself just so she could touch him, so she could knock him to earth and squat on his chest, teasing open the buttons of his shirt until he giggled and wriggled out from under her.

Three

Duets with a Minotaur

They continued their journey and at length arrived at a river, a writhing torrent scored with rapids, too swift to swim, and they paced the banks seeking a bottleneck or rocks they might step over and soon came to what they'd least expected, a bridge, arched as the rainbows flecking the spray beneath it, built of pieced stone, moss tracing the mortar. At the foot of the bridge, on a close-cropped lawn, stood a small tower, also of stone, slate-tiled, and before the tower a queer being sat on a stool holding a frying pan above a fire. The creature had a bull's head, black, with horns scything like a sickle moon from the knoll above its eyes and a gold hoop in its nostrils. But below the neck it was formed like a man, resplendently appareled in a white shirt ruffled at the throat, a scarlet coat and black trousers. At its side a sword pommeled in ivory slanted in a silver scabbard.

The fears of the robbers still echoing in his ears, Pico trembled a little as they approached the tower and its tenant but the beast set the pan at the edge of the fire, rose and bowed gravely, greeting them in a voice rich as blood, deep as a root.

"Good morning, travelers," he said. "My name is Balquo. I am the bridgekeeper and would be delighted should you join me for breakfast," and as the scent lifting from the frying pan was fabulous, they agreed. The minotaur fetched two more stools and a small round table from the tower and set the table with a linen cloth and silver cutlery and glazed stoneware. A pot gurgling on the coals contained coffee which he strained into their mugs and then served each a whole fresh trout, fried with mushrooms, garnished with wild fennel and half a lime.

The trout was light and sweet as the mist sifting off the river and they ate without speaking, listening to the batter and dash of the water as it sped beneath the bridge. Then, while Pico and Adevi rolled cigarettes, the beast refilled their mugs, leaned back against a doorpost and said, "After a hearty breakfast, over my second cup of coffee, I like to hear a story if there's one at hand. Would you be so good as to oblige me?"

"I don't tell stories in daylight," Adevi scowled but Pico leaned forward. He told of his quest, of his hope of finding the morning town, of his journey into the forest, of his capture by the robbers and training as a thief and of Adevi's decision to accompany him. The minotaur nodded solemnly when he was done.

"I have lived here a long time, mongrels such as I do not age as you purebreds do. Several times I have met those who searched for the morning town, young men or women bent on attaining wings."

"And did they reach it?" Pico cried. "Did they come to the school for flying?"

"None has ever crossed this bridge while I have guarded it," the minotaur replied, "and I do not know what lies on the other side."

"Is it forbidden to cross the bridge?" Adevi asked.

"It is not forbidden but all who wish to cross must first do battle with me. I am the bridgekeeper and I have never lost a fight."

Crestfallen, Pico asked, "Is there no other way across the river?"

"This river is the border of the deep forest and none may cross it save by this bridge. But come, guests, do not look so disheartened. You need not cross the bridge yet or indeed at any time. I would prefer you stayed here to keep me company as the business of bridgekeeping is a lonely affair. There are trout in the river and mushrooms and rabbits in the woods. We could sing in the evenings and play games of checkers and the fishing is fine sport."

"I, at least, must cross the bridge or die in the attempt," said Pico. "I will not forsake my quest. But first, if you will, sir, your own story."

The minotaur sighed and ran his hands along his horns.

"Once, in the city by the sea," he began, "lived a girl called Yani, gorgeous as a fire, and she loved to wander. Her father was a merchant, a stern man, and he hired three nurses to look after her, but she always escaped, scampering willy-nilly across the hills and into the forest fringes. The nurses, when they caught her, told tales of the beasts that lived there.

"'They'll eat you up from the inside out,' they scolded but Yani only danced a wild dance, chanting, 'Eat me up from the inside out, eat me up from the inside out.' The nurses clucked and shook their haggard heads.

"One morning Yani ventured farther into the forest than ever before and soon was lost, staggering among trunks, battling branches and brambles, briars snagging her dress. She cried, prying at the thorns, but they only clung closer and soon she crouched making the small moans of an animal in agony. After a while she looked up and saw a black bull coming toward her and she thrashed and howled but the bull fixed her with such a solemn stare that she quieted and allowed him to unravel the brambles with his horns. Then he licked away her tears with his tongue of sand and led her to a clearing where they cavorted in sunlight and she made necklaces of anemones to fix about his neck and tied her hair ribbons to his horns. They danced in wild places till dawn and then he led her back to the edge of the forest. Though she cajoled he would not leave the trees and watched her until she vanished into the city streets.

"The next day she slipped her nurses' clutches once again and the bull was waiting at the edge of the forest. He showed her secret places in the woods and they frolicked and made love and napped till late afternoon, her head on his flank, hand on his horn.

"On the third day, alerted by the nurses, Yani's father allowed her to escape but followed at a distance. When he saw a bull emerge from the trees he pulled the bow from his shoulder and loosed an arrow into the beast's heart. The bull fell, his blood making black flowers on his coat, his eyes never leaving Yani's face, and she clutched his massive neck, sobbing as the contents of his heart soaked her breast. Her father had to fetch assistance to pry her from the dead beast's body.

"After that she sat despondent, staring at the sea, tears pooling in her cupped palms and in the chambers of her heart as well, until she learned she was pregnant. Then she capered about the house clapping her hands and would have shouted the tidings in the streets but her irate father battened her in the highest tower where she stayed, gleeful as a dolphin, for nine months while her belly swelled.

"On a morning as reckless as a dust devil the child was born, feetfirst.

"'A boy,' the nurses cried, then fainted in a heap as the rest of the body slid out. Yani, with the end of her strength, cut the cord and lifted the baby to her breast, counting its fingers and toes, feebly fondling its soft nose and tiny horns. She named it, kissed it and then she died, for a girl's body is not made for the birthing of a beast.

"Her father's anger dissolved at the death of his daughter and he did not do away with his grandson but raised him in secret, schooling him with private tutors sworn to silence. When the creature was a young man the grandfather searched for him a position outside the home but away from the eyes of the city dwellers, for he knew their loathing of deviation.

"The post of bridgekeeper had recently fallen vacant, the previous guard having grown old, and so the half-breed was sent into the forest to live out his days as guardian of the deep woods.

"And here I sit awaiting errant folk such as yourselves, to dissuade them from their journey or do battle if need be. It is not a bad life for one misborn, though a lonely one. Once a year I receive a new suit of clothes and supplies of coffee, salt and other necessities from the city but otherwise I have no contact with my birthplace unless travelers arrive."

.   .   .

Behind the tower the minotaur tilled a garden irrigated by the gusting mist off the river and the morning dew. That afternoon Pico knelt with him weeding between the rows and he told Balquo of his time with the robbers, all of whom had been banished from the city by choice or by deed.

"Yes, the forest gathers the between people," Balquo said, "those uneasy in the straitjackets of normalcy."

"Oh why could I not accept my lot?" Pico said. "Why could I not be content in the city by the sea?"

"Are any content?" the minotaur pondered morosely. "I've met many who wandered here from the seashore and all were searching, searching."

"I was content once, or so I like to think. When I was with my winged girl she loved the stories I told, I loved to see her fly."

"What about Adevi. Is she happy?"

"I asked her once. She's happy, she told me, when she's stealing. But her heart is hidden, who can tell?"

Adevi had strung her bow and gone to stalk game. Now she returned with a brace of partridges. She pulled a stool to the edge of the garden and plucked and gutted the birds, entertaining them with such a chilling tale as she worked that Pico did not know whether to believe it, though he knew what she was capable of. Balquo was fascinated.

"You're the first thief I've met in these parts," he told her, "though I've heard rumors of your band, even of a girl robber, fiercest of them all."

"You're looking at her," Adevi grinned as she ripped the head off the second bird, her cheek peppered with blood.

The minotaur was an excellent cook. He stewed the partridges in a sauce of wild plums, boiled new potatoes in their skins and strewed them with fresh parsley while Pico made a salad from the garden, dousing it with vinegar and olive oil from crystal cruets. They ate as night rose and afterward the minotaur smoked a pipe and doled out tots of blackberry brandy while Pico and Adevi lit cigarettes. Adevi asked Pico to read from his books. He read a story and when he was done Balquo clamored for another so he sat silent awhile, then closed the book and told the following:

"After many years away a man returned to the town of his birth bearing a box the size of a child's coffin, of wood and unadorned. The children milled about him, plucked at his trousers as he paced the dusty streets, for strangers seldom came to the town, and they pleaded to know what the box contained.

"'That is my secret,' the man said, 'which I shall never reveal.'

"His father and mother had long since died and the house where he'd lived as a boy was empty as a broken pot, the rooms silted with dust, timbers tilting, so the next days he spent setting the boards straight, fixing the doors, sweeping the floor. He bought a few cups and plates, some stools and a bed, and he placed the box on a table in the center of the largest room. Friends from childhood arrived to welcome him and he served them tea as they reminisced about the games they'd played, about the people they'd known who'd died, and then they asked what he'd brought from his journeys, what the box contained.

"'That is my secret,' the man told them, 'which I shall never reveal,' and his guests left discontented and returned to their families grumbling about the airs adopted by those who'd traveled abroad.

"He found work as a baker's assistant, laboring all night shirtless before the yellow maw of the oven in the good odor of bread and the ladies of the town contrived excuses to buy their loaves from his shop, for travelers and secrets will always summon the women.

"Now the baker's daughter was a comely lass, hair the color of wheat, breasts like risen rolls, and she cajoled him to take her strolling in the evenings before he went to work. He spoke little but it pleased her to be seen on the boulevards with this man and his mantle of mystery. She took his arm and chattered and he nodded sometimes though his thoughts seemed always elsewhere.

"After half a year of such promenades she asked him whether he wouldn't ask her father for her hand and at this he lifted the object in question, stroked her fingers and said, 'I will marry you if first you hear a tale and then agree to heed a demand.'

"He led her to a park bench near a fountain. His voice barely audible above the water's tumble, he told her of a distant city at the far end of his travels where he'd had two friends, a young man who studied astronomy and a young woman, 'beautiful as yourself,' he said, 'though her hair was the color of the sunset. Sometimes the three of us would carry a picnic of cold meats, bread and wine through a trapdoor in the ceiling of the astronomer's apartment and sit all night with his brass telescope spying on the planets and musing on who might dwell in those far worlds. The astronomer, though a genius, was half mad, and had devised plans for a craft powered by cobwebs that would take him and a companion to the moon and beyond. We teased him and clamored to be his travel mate but he was in earnest and said we would draw lots when the time came. Meanwhile we were to save up the cobwebs we swept from the corners of our rooms. We listened to him, delirious on his dreams and too much wine, as he told of the distances between the stars, which may only be measured in the lifetimes of mountains. At dawn the girl and I descended to the street to drink coffee but the astronomer stayed in his room scribbling equations, giddy with the enigmas of the heavens.

" 'The girl was a cellist who, much to the delight of passersby, practiced naked on her balcony, claiming the contact of the wood with her flesh embellished the tone and all who heard agreed. One night she brought her instrument to a rooftop star session and played as we lay on our backs and the astronomer commented that not only did her music echo the movements of the stars, it seemed to affect them.

" 'Over time the girl and I became lovers. We always laughed about our friend the mad astronomer, speaking about him as one might speak of a precocious child or a pet monkey. He seldom left his apartment so if we wanted to see him we would have to visit, always at night, for night is necessarily the realm of the astronomer, as well as that of the baker and the poet and the thief.

" 'I worked in that city as a dealer in antiques, my house filled with receptacles of old memories, and sometimes my trade took me to outlying districts where I'd spend a day or two before returning to my house. One day I returned earlier than expected and in the evening went to the girl's room but she was out so I walked to the astronomer's apartment. The door was unlocked and his ladder lay against the open trapdoor so I climbed out among the stars and found my two friends twined naked on the tiles, telescope and cello lying to either side.'

" 'What did you do?' the baker's daughter asked.

"'I left that city and walked for many months until I arrived again at this town where I had begun my journey.'

"'Carrying your box.'

"'Yes, carrying my box.' He pressed her hand. 'You have heard my tale. Now listen to my demand. I will be a good husband to you if you swear one thing, that you allow me an hour a day alone with my box and that you never ask what it contains or try to look for yourself.'

"It seemed a simple enough request and she agreed, so the man asked the baker for his daughter's hand and one month later they married.

"As promised the man proved a good husband, never shirking his duties, and the baker was pleased to acquire such a hardworking son-in-law. He was much like the other husbands of the town, perhaps a little more gentle in bed, perhaps more pensive, but every afternoon he locked his wife out of the house to be alone for an hour with his box.

"It may seem an easy task to disregard a secret but secrets are like splinters beneath the flesh, the infection spreads and spreads and then the limb turns gangrenous and must be sawn away, all for the sake of a sliver of wood. At first the new bride was delighted with her man and the daily hour of banishment seemed sweet punishment in return for the bliss, but the box was always between them and slowly it swelled enormous in her mind and she could not think, could not sleep, could not be easy in her husband's presence because of what he kept from her. So one day instead of walking to the house of a friend as was usual in her hour of exile, she turned back and peeked through the keyhole and saw her husband bending over the open box, weeping as though a wall had fallen inside him. Of course she could not rest until she knew what caused her love such pain. That very night while he was away baking she lifted the box lid and saw within it a heap of bones and a skull and to the skull still clung filaments of flame-colored hair.

"She ran shrieking through the streets of the town and her husband, knowing that voice, left the bread to scorch and dashed all floury back to the house where the box lay open upon the table.

"By the time the woman had settled enough to tell what she had seen and a bevy of men armed with hoes and pitchforks had arrived at the house simmering with righteous rage the traveler had gone and the box with him. Though they followed his tracks through the dust out of town at first light they could not catch him and at noon a wind blew up and pulled the footprints after it into the sky, into the sky where the stars lay hidden."

The minotaur plucked a coal from the fire with bronze tongs to light his pipe, which had gone out.

"Why must we murder those we love?" he said. "How many young girls have sat with me beside this tower and some, though you may not believe it, have lain with me, half beast that I am, and I have stroked their hair, served them my finest dishes, offered them a life of indolence here beside this tower, but always in the end they desired the unknown across the river over contentment on this bank. Though they knew they'd die at my hand, they had to try to cross. Oh why was this task given me?"

"Can't you just let them go?" Adevi asked. "What's to stop you letting a few across?"

Balquo shook his head solemnly. "This is my duty," he said. "I will not shirk it."

"I too have murdered every man I loved," said Adevi complacently. "Because in the end the pleasure of entering flesh was greater than that of being entered, and there were always more men."

Pico turned to Balquo. "Have you ever killed someone and not felt remorse, have you known the pleasure Adevi claims coexists with murder?"

"Certainly," the minotaur replied and the rest of that evening he and Adevi traded vignettes of slayings, vying to describe the daintiest knife work, the worthiest opponent, and Pico listened aghast as the tales grew grandiose, blood mounting on blood as the level of brandy in the bottle receded.

When at last they stumbled away from the remains of the fire Adevi followed Pico and laid her blanket beside his at the far end of the sward but he said, "I want to be alone tonight, Adevi. Go to Balquo. He's lonely for a woman and surely here at last is the man you've yearned for, beast enough to satisfy your desires, sufficiently gentle to tame your waywardness. I saw how his eyes hung on your body. Go to him, Adevi."

So that night the thief's shouts and minotaur's bellows boomed in the tower while Pico grinned and tried to get some sleep. They rose at noon and Balquo sang at the top of his voice while he prepared a monstrous brunch but Pico realized with dismay that Adevi's thirsty stare was unquenched, her eyes stayed not on the minotaur's bulk but on himself, reproachful, and she did not finish her plate.

That afternoon they played croquet on the lawn, taking care not to lose the balls over the embankment, and in the evening Balquo taught the poet several roundelays which they sang as duets, Pico's thin tenor like a trimming of raw silk about the broadcloth of Balquo's bass.

The days passed swiftly as the river between the banks, the surface sparkling, but beneath the glitter and spray, like dark fish tapering into and out of shadows, the knowledge of the inevitable crossing of the bridge slid.

Most mornings Pico rose at dawn, fetched a bamboo rod from the tower and sat on a tuft of grass fishing. Later Balquo would join him there, flinging the line into the stream, plucking the trout like the iridescent gobbets on the end of a glassblower's pipe to dull on the grass behind them. The minotaur's conversation was all about Adevi.

"I've never known a woman like her. Holding her is like trying to embrace a cornered boar." He unbuttoned his coat to display wounds on his chest, which he'd stanched with dry moss. "I didn't know she'd hurt me till I saw the blood on the sheets," he chuckled. "She loves my horns. On top of me, she holds them like handles as though I were a plow she guided. Last night I was spent and so she told me to lie still and straddled my head, impaling herself on a horn. And when we're through lovemaking she tickles my back with the tip of her knife and tells me bedtime stories gruesome enough to blanch onyx. Are they true, the stories she tells?"

"Nothing I've seen or heard of her life has given me cause to doubt them."

"Ah, poet, the months and years I've dreamed of women here in this forgotten outpost. I thought there was no permutation I'd not meditated on but clearly my brain lacked the courage to imagine Adevi."

"Yes," said Pico sadly, "sometimes our desires are not evident until they land on our doorsteps."

"Will she stay do you think, Pico? Will she stay with me?"

"I don't know. She's a wildfire and taming a fire's tricky. She needs fuel to burn and if she doesn't burn she'll flicker out. But I believe you could tame her. You have horns. Horns don't burn."

To leave the lovers room alone Pico took to wandering far up or down the riverbank with his notebook. He loved especially the dusk when he was sad with the exquisite sadness of memory's restlessness, when the water turned to metal and the swallows slashed the remaining light to shreds.

The writing of poetry is a chancy business, its currency solitude and loss, its tools coffee and too much wine, its hours midnight, dawn and dusk, and unlike other trades the hours asleep are not time off. Pico paced the banks and sat to write a line or word and paced again and sometimes a poem arrived whole and being a poet seemed the easiest work in the world. Other times he wrestled for a day with one word, he's pinned, shoulder blades to earth, it has him in a choke hold and he goes to sleep certain he'll wake an imbecile from lack of blood to the brain but in the morning he can flick the word away like a pesky gnat and pick from a swarm of others circling his head, drawn by the ferment, the phrases composting in his skull. But though a poem might seem marvelous during its composition, upon rereading he was always dissatisfied, the vision unachieved.

One evening Adevi came to him as he walked alone muttering and he startled.

"Why do you wander by yourself?" she asked.

"Twilight is the hour I love," he told her, "the hour where nothing is quite itself, all things teetering at the edges of their names. Here I can be alone and a stranger to myself."

"I'm a fire," said Adevi, "fires burn brightest at night," but her voice was small and she didn't look at him.

"What's wrong, Adevi?"

"Poet, why have you forsaken me?"

"Aren't you happy with Balquo?"

"Balquo makes me shout like no other but that's no answer to my question. Why have you forsaken me? What in me repulses you?"

"Adevi, you're the strongest woman I've ever met but I'm in love with another."

"But we were together."

"If I'd stayed with you longer, Adevi, I'd have been eaten, I'd have ended up a husk."

"I can change. I can leave off killing, I can learn to cook, I can wear dresses."

"I don't want you to change."

"You think I'm ugly," she cried, mauling her hair.

"No, Adevi, please. You're beautiful, you know you are, I've told you so."

"Then why won't you have me?"

"Why do you want me? I'm a weakling, my arms have the muscles of a mushroom, I have no taste for blood, you've said yourself I'm the most inept fighter you've ever seen. We have nothing in common. Balquo adores you, he has what I lack, what you desire, go to him."

But she began to weep, not as a girl weeps but in the great groaning sobs of men's crying, each moan hauled out against her will.

"Stop, Adevi," Pico said, tears in his eyes as well. "Why are you doing this to yourself?"

"Love me, poet," she moaned, "love me."

"I can't."

Then she drew her knife, sending him to the ground with the edge of her arm and kneeling on his shoulders, one hand holding his head back, the other pressing the blade to his neck. In her eyes he saw an anguish that mirrored the sorrow in his own heart. "Do it, Adevi," he said. "I'm unhappy as well. Send me to the place of forgetting where your other lovers have gone, your knife can free me from my torment and free you from me, kill me, Adevi." But she sheathed the blade and stroked his cheeks with her rough fingers and tears fell from her eyes into his and smarted there as if they were hotter or saltier than his own. Then she got up and walked away, through the leaves that revolved in the twilight like a sparse dark rain.

Next morning after breakfast Pico pushed back his stool and stood.

"Who would have imagined," he said, "that one on such a journey could have found such hospitality where it was least expected. Balquo, you have a heart equal to your girth. These past days have been an eye of serenity in the tempest of my travels, a time of tales and re-flection. I have partaken of your culinary genius and drunk your ex-cellent brandy. Adevi, you released me from the robber camp and guided me to this place and taught me your trade though I was never your finest student. I have nothing to offer you good people in return for your gifts save my stories and some advice. I believe that if I have served a purpose in your lives it was to bring you two together. Never have I met two people who complemented each other as you do and I sense that if you stayed together you would find heartsease, here by the river, bridgekeeper and thief.

"As for myself, it's time I was moving on, more than ever my desire is to find the morning town and the house of my hopes. Though I know there is little chance of defeating you, Balquo, I must try. The way to my love lies eastward."

The minotaur looked glum but he stood and faced Pico.

"Are you certain I cannot convince you to forsake your journey, your adherence to a tale that is at best a myth, at worst a delusion di-recting you to death? We have become friends, poet, you and I. Why not stay in this place which you have admitted provides solace, and space for your work. Will you not reconsider?"

Pico spread his hands. "I must find my wings or die in the at-tempt."

Balquo sighed and nodded. He entered the tower and returned with a dusty bottle in one hand and a long slim rosewood box in the other. He set the bottle on the table, uncorked it, and champagne bloomed over his fist.

"It is my custom," he said, "to toast my combatant before the fight," and he poured three glasses of wine frothy as the river water and they tinkled the glasses together. "May the best man win," Balquo said and they drained the champagne. Then he placed the box on the table, unclasped the lid and lifted it to reveal an array of rapiers on violet velvet, all in a state of impeccable glitter. As Pico bent over the box to choose his weapon, Adevi suddenly stood, knocking over her stool, and walked toward the bridge.

"Stop," cried the minotaur, leaping to the foot of the bridge, but she drew her falchion and lunged at him and he was compelled to snatch his own weapon from its scabbard and parry the blow.

"No, Adevi," Pico cried, "this is my task," but she shouted back as she forced the minotaur out over the water, "I believe you, Pico, I believe in the morning town, I believe you'll get your wings, I believe . . ."

So Pico watched horrified as the two teetered across the spit of stone above the spinning waters. Both were consummate fighters, feet fleet as dragonflies, blades steel tongues licking, and soon both were sliced and the already slick surface of the bridge grew treacherous with blood. Balquo's bulk often forced Adevi to scurry backward, frantically fending off blows with her notched knife, but the thief's agility allowed her under the minotaur's slower thrusts and once she even slipped between his legs. As the fight lengthened it took on a rhythm as though the duelists waltzed in the sunlight on the bridge, as though they acted toward some common purpose, and though his guts squirmed at the sight of the wounds yet Pico was also able to delight in their artistry.

Eventually the minotaur, more used to battling on this slender span, wore Adevi down and Pico watched aghast as her parries grew weaker. At last Balquo moved in to deal the deathblow. He looked up a moment before he struck though and his beast's eyes knocked on her emerald glance, a fatal hesitation, for with the last of her strength Adevi flung herself onto his sword, rushed up it till she met the hilt with her belly, and drove her knife into the bull neck. Together they toppled off the bridge and the river received the bodies without checking its clamor. Pico fainted.

The spray of the river revived him and he sat up and stared dully at the aluminum buckling of the water and his desire was to cast himself into its rush, into the torrent that had taken his friends. The area about Balquo's tower seemed so empty he almost felt he himself was absent. As though the space Balquo and Adevi had inhabited was greater than the air they displaced and their departure had sucked the world dry. How easy it would be, he thought, to release his hold on this grass and slip down the bank. But he heard Adevi's final cry, "I believe," and knew her death had tied him to his difficult destiny.

Pico washed the dishes. He carried water from the river and scrupulously scrubbed the knives and forks and cups, the breakfast plates, the frying pan and coffeepot, and rinsed and dried them and replaced them in the cupboard in the tower where Balquo had kept his kitchenware. Then he swept the tower and made the bed, touching sorrowfully the damp residue of lovemaking, the drying trace of the union of a thief and a minotaur. Lastly he filled his knapsack with supplies, taking salt and flour and coffee and a stoppered bottle of oil from Balquo's larder, a few potatoes and carrots from the garden, and from Adevi's possessions he added tobacco and cigarette papers, her bow and quiver. The afternoon was well advanced by the time he'd finished his preparations but he knew he could not stay another night in this sough of memories, so he shouldered his pack and without a backward glance walked across the bridge and into the forest beyond.

In the deep forest the trees grew larger. As he made his way eastward over the next days he noticed that the trunks, which had been huge before, now lifted like cliff faces and the roof of leaves was far loftier. This swelling of his surroundings had two effects. One was to ease the claustrophobia, the sense of encroaching arms that had tormented him before. Though the shadows remained the twilight now hung like an alternate sky, so vast it seemed. The other effect was to open out the undergrowth so he now walked easier, in a vast temple of corroded pillars, misshapen porticoes, pediments mosaicked in lichen, the colonnades floored in a carpet of leaves woven over millennia.

He did not weep for a week and then he wept for three days as though the tears had slowly lifted inside him till the tide overtopped his eyelids. He wept for three days sitting beside a dead fire, slowly rubbing cold ashes into his skin, his hair. On the night of the third day he met Balquo and Adevi in a dream. They were walking together along the riverbank holding hands and he said, "But I thought you were dead," and Adevi smiled at him and said, "No, we're here." When he woke in the morning he went to a nearby brook and washed the ashes from his body.

It was some time before the conversations with Balquo and Adevi, especially Adevi, died down. It seemed his ear did not need their voices nearby to hear them and often as he walked, as he ate, as he fetched firewood or hunted, he found he was chatting.

"What is courage?" he asked, and Adevi replied, "Courage is the swallowing of one's life, whole."

When he read in the evenings he looked up to share a sentence with them but they weren't there and when he wrote a verse he liked he wanted to read it to them but they weren't there, weren't there.

Now he put to use the skills Adevi had taught him, stalking hares and pigeons among the obelisks of light, and though he lacked her accuracy he was never without meat if he wanted it. But he could not relish the release of blood as she had. He never killed without remorse for the leaps left in a hare's legs, a dove's flight curtailed.

He traveled twenty-two days after the crossing of the bridge, among ever greater trees, the walking becoming ever easier. He talked often with the memory of his friends and he wished always to meet another traveler.

Four

Master Rabbit's Tale

Night, and a storm was striding toward him, its giant footsteps quaking the earth, shaking branches down, and he sought shelter by the spasms of violet light, a hollow in a trunk or a grotto where he could cower for a few hours, but no such nook presented itself. The first wave of rain instantly drenched him and he thought he'd have to simply crouch beside a big tree and hope no toppling bough banged him into eternity when he saw by one of the flares what looked like a small door set in a low hill. The darkness clapped shut again but he struggled up to the door and pounded upon it with his fists.

"Sanctuary," he shouted above the wind. "Sanctuary," and waited so long he was about to try the lock but then the brass knob turned and the door swung open. The moment before he stooped to enter, a spray of lightning illuminated a sign above the lintel. MASTER RABBIT, it read in letters burned into a strip of wood.

He stumbled into the color a traveler cherishes above all others, the yellow of lamplight, of indoor firelight. In the abrupt stillness he took off his hat and with his sleeve dashed the rain from his eyes and looked up to find himself in a round room with a fire snapping in a hearth at the far end, a whistling teakettle hooked above the flames. On a braided rug beside the fire stood two rocking chairs with quilted cushions tied to their seats. Around the walls cases and shelves contained heaps and rows of objects, birds' nests and blown eggs, pressed leaves, pinned beetles and butterflies, the fluted houses of wasps, sheaves of dried grasses, jars filled with colored earths, rocks on kapok in chambered boxes, each object tagged with a strip of paper on which was scribbled a name and number. In one corner was a large wicker cage, empty. And also to his astonishment and delight he saw several shelves of leather-bound books.

Now his curious host turned from locking the door, Master Rabbit to be sure, tenant of this warm den, wearing a brown turtleneck sweater and a scuffed gray coat, half-moon spectacles on his nose and, incongruously, a lovely flower hooked over one of his lop ears in the manner of young girls, though this specimen still had the roots attached, trailing on the disheveled coat collar. The rabbit bustled up to Pico muttering, "Ah, you're wet through. Here, set your knapsack against the wall and let's get those clothes off you." Pico stripped to his shorts and dried himself on a proffered towel then shrugged into the bathrobe the rabbit held for him.

"No night for walking," the rabbit said. "No indeed, just the sort of weather that might bring on a nasty chest cold. But we'll steam the chill out of you. Come," he patted the seat of a rocker. "Make yourself comfortable." Pico sank into the chair with a groan of ecstasy and let the rabbit place his feet on a stool and tuck a blanket about them.

"Now," said the rabbit, "how does a mug of hot tea with a mite of rum sound?"

"Oh lovely, lovely," sighed Pico, unable to believe that five minutes before he'd been tramping in a tempest. And here he was being served tea and rum by a bespectacled bunny with a flower in his ear.

"I'll be just a minute," his host said, "you drink that slowly," so Pico sipped the scalding tea and stared drowsily at the fire while the rabbit clattered and mumbled in a room deeper into the hill. In a few minutes he returned with a bowl of oatmeal porridge sprinkled with brown sugar and cinnamon, swimming in cream.

"Am I dreaming?" Pico asked as he took the bowl.

The rabbit looked up in earnest surprise. "Oh I shouldn't think so. Unless of course I am as well, which I'm fairly sure is not the case. But perhaps my existence has been a product of your imagination and you chose this wild night to come see how your figment is progressing. Did you?"

"Of course not," Pico laughed.

"Well, then, I believe we are both awake. And in that case introductions are in order. I am, should you have missed the signboard outside, Master Rabbit, and this is my humble warren. You are welcome."

"Thank you ever so much. My name is Pico. I was once a librarian in the city by the sea but am now a lonesome traveler making my way through the forest to the morning town of Paunpuam beyond its eastern edge and there I hope to receive wings that I might gain the love of a beautiful girl."

Master Rabbit had also taken up a mug of tea and now sat on the other rocker, feet some distance above the floor. He set down his cup and ransacked his coat until he came up with a pencil stub and a square of folded paper on which he carefully wrote the poet's name and checked with Pico for spelling. After gazing at it some moments he tucked it into an inner pocket, then cast about for his teacup. Pico bent and placed it in his hands.

"Thank you, thank you, young Pico. Countless storms have blown countless waifs and strays to my door, some even more bedraggled than you, but I do not believe I have ever received a guest from the city by the sea. Is it far?"

"I've been traveling now in fits and starts for well-nigh two months."

"I see. A fair distance. And I have never strayed more than a day's journey from my home here in the center of the woods." He peered at Pico through the crescents of thick glass.

Pico said, "Who, I mean, if you will pardon my inquisitiveness, what are you? What do you do here? You're not like the other rabbits I've met."

"No, I dare say not," the rabbit twisted an ear bashfully. "I am, well, you might call me a guardian, a keeper, a keeper of the forest, or perhaps just a forester would do. Yes, a forester. You noticed my collections as you came in?" and Pico nodded eagerly.

"They're fascinating."

"Indeed. Well, that is my labor, such as it is, the garnering and preserving of knowledge." He waved a hand at shelves cluttered with quartz crystals, soil samples, fossil worms. "Why, just before your arrival I was examining a specimen gathered this afternoon, a rare flower, the first I've seen of its type, now where did I put it? This house is so full, you see," he glanced apologetically at Pico, who gently lifted the blossom from the rabbit's ear. The forester looked at the poet in astonishment.

"Ah yes, there it is. Curious how they wander around, these objects, they have their little games, but anyway take a look here, you can see the star-shaped sepal and here the double-twisted ovary, quite unusual."

"It's beautiful," said Pico.

The rabbit looked up at him then back down at the flower, eyes wide.

"Yes," he said. "Yes it is, you're quite right." He held it at arm's length, nodding earnestly till Pico asked, "Where did you get your books?"

"Get them?"

"Where are they from? Did you buy them?"

"Oh. I wrote them."

"You wrote them?"

"Indeed. Look." And he stood on the rocker, overbalanced, caught himself and tipped down a tome which he handed to Pico. A careful script filled each page, infrequently relieved by drawings of leaves and seedpods and sections of trunks. Pico read several lines of intricate commentary on the life cycle of a certain parasite of a certain tree, then flipped forward. More of the same. Brown ink clogged with jargon, the delicate drawings, some with a smudging of color across them, each figure numbered.

"Are there no stories?" Pico asked.

"Stories?" The rabbit looked baffled.

"Is there nothing one would read for pleasure, for the joy of reading?"

"My books are not written for entertainment, young traveler, but for edification," the rabbit said in an admonitory tone. "Did you think I spent my time scribbling amorous adventures when there was work to be done?"

"What work?"

"Why, the task of detailing the known world, the habits of flora and fauna, the intricacies of geology."

"But to what end?"

"Knowledge, dear boy, knowledge. How can we live in a world we do not comprehend?"

Pico leafed through the book a little sadly. "Some of the drawings are pretty," he said, "but they seem so distant from what a tree is, from that rustling musculature which says words if you listen closely enough."

"The interior is always at odds with what is seen from the outside," the forester nodded. "When you have learned the name of every part of a plant or beast, learned the function of each vein, each strand of chlorophyll, when you have heard the twitter of each nerve and felt the twitch of each root hair, felt the shedding of skin, bark and scale, the churn of the heart and the turn of the leaf to the sunlight, why, then that object is yours to command. I am master of the forest. I have lived in these woods a very long time, indeed since the forest was saplings, wandering in the slow growth of the trees, uncovering the secrets they held, learning their names."

"I work with names as well," Pico said. "I am not a namer but a renamer. In my art I arrive at the nature of a thing by calling it something else. The sky is the sea glittering with minnows caught in the nets of the rain, a flute at dusk is a lover's tongue in the ear, an eye is a talon, a cinder, a star."

"But then you have failed to clarify, failed to illumine the marvelous workings of the eye, the focusing lens of the retina, the rods and cones, the cord that carries colors to the brain."

"Yes, the mystery stays intact but the spirit is sensed."

The rabbit peered at Pico, taken aback, then began a discourse on logical thought. But following the slog in the storm and the hot tea and rum and the milky porridge, Pico's lids inexorably drooped and a moment later the rabbit was shaking his shoulder and berating himself. "A terrible host," he was saying, "gabbling away and you're exhausted. It's been so long since I had anyone to talk to, you see. Come, come, we must get you to bed." He bundled Pico off the rocking chair and led him through a blur of other rooms all small and round and dark to one which held a hole in the wall, a cocoon, into which Pico crawled and was instantly asleep.

He woke in the same darkness, in soft fur, and knew he'd slept for ages by the way his dreams still struggled for handholds in his brain. Dreams of rabbits. He was a long time remembering he lay indeed in the depths of a rabbit hole. He stretched and touched the sides of the hollow that smelled of earth and roots and rabbit, then tumbled out and followed a thread of light through several rooms till he arrived at one where his host sat before a massive desk silted with papers, papers sifting to the floor around him, peering at a seed through a magnifying glass.

"Good morning," said Pico and the rabbit jumped. "Oh," he said, "you're awake. And how did you sleep?"

"If I'd woken any later I'd have become part of the hill," Pico yawned.

"Excellent. Your breakfast is waiting through that door. I must work today, I have cataloging to do, but the house is yours, you are welcome to peruse my collection at your leisure."

On a table flanked by a stool Pico found a teakettle under a cozy, a brown mug, a soft-boiled egg in an eggcup and under a cloth a plate of scones. Two ceramic pots held butter and orange marmalade. The flower that the forester had lodged behind his ear now stood in a jar in the center of the table. As Pico ate he looked around the room at the still lifes stacked on the shelves. In crafting order the forester had unwittingly spawned beauty, the sequenced minerals in their cases, the pinned butterflies, the delicate hues of grasses were like collages, their colors shimmering. He read several tags hoping for an explanation of their beauty but the slips of paper contained names that bore no relation, musical or visual, to their antecedents.

Master Rabbit's house meandered into the hillside the way a pumpkin vine creeps, sending tendrils this way and that, the globed rooms spilling to either side. Carrying a candle, Pico moved through them examining the collections. Rooms of bones and rooms of feathers, rooms of seedpods and rooms of beetles. Everywhere a smell that reminded him of his library, an odor of dust and stagnant knowledge. The uneven walls of the rooms had been whitewashed and like petrified worms pale roots reached through cracks, forking to water and finding only stale air.

He came at last back into the room with the fireplace and there sat till lunchtime browsing through the books the rabbit had written, reading the stately sapless prose carefully scribed in copperplate, dense with figures and botanical names. And in that quiet house, reading of the strange habits of flora and fauna, with the rustle of turning pages and the dry bracken scent of old paper, he could almost imagine himself back in his library.

Sometime after noon the rabbit called him to lunch. They carried a cloth and cushions outside and laid a picnic under a tree, beside an upright slab of gray stone bedded in the grass. The rabbit had made a salad of spinach, radishes, tomatoes, olives, carrots and cucumbers, all popping fresh, served from a wooden bowl with a bottle of red wine and slices off a loaf of black bread he modestly admitted he'd baked himself. The storm had scrubbed the sky to a porcelain blue and filled the air with the green smell of glad grass, the juicy tang of snapped twigs. When they finished the meal the rabbit put his paws behind his head and leaned back against the trunk, whiskers wine-stained, and Pico as well lay back and lit a cigarette. The afternoon felt huge, a warm ocean lapping at his skin. His smoke rings teetered and ruptured among the leaves.

"Your books," said Pico, "they do have stories in them. At first I thought them bland, but as I read on I began to hear the stories, the wanton births and deaths, the zany couplings, the cruel devouring of children by parents, of lovers by loved ones."

"I write only the facts," said the forester, "the stories are incidental."

"Stories are life," protested Pico. "Without them, books would be only paper and ink, with them they breathe, the reader is drawn in, the stories become him."

"The stories become him," the rabbit muttered, a ruby oblong tossed by the surface of the wine wavering on his chin. "The stories become him. You like stories, young traveler. I will tell you a story.

"You may believe me utterly content here in the center of the woods, a naturalist surrounded by the objects of his attentions, and indeed for the most part I am, but I have been lonely, yes, I have been lonely.

"Though my concern is generally with the inanimate, one night, as I was laboring over my lists of names, I heard a voice. Once in a lifetime a voice arrives at one's hearing that speaks not to the mind but to the blood and I went outside and stood listening to a song from the branches of a tree, of this tree we sit beneath. That night was so bright. I stared through the spaces in the leaves and, my mind still engaged with words, read the images made of moon and breeze. Shoals of pale fish, faces shadowed, gaping, winking, arcane symbols constantly erased and redrawn. And at the center of all a nightingale sang a song that broke my heart. Had I been able to accept the gift of that song and return to my scribbling perhaps I would not have acquired the burden of sadness that now weighs on me. But greed overwhelmed my rational brain and I had to own that song.

"I had within my rooms various traps and snares with which I occasionally captured the creatures of the forest in order to further my research. I fetched one of these, a simple noose, and placed it on the ground, a saucer of honey within its circle. Then I went to sleep, the song still throbbing like a sweet wound in my brain.

"I woke early and came to this tree, to the spot where I had set the snare and found, caught by a tiny ankle, not the slender feathered husk I'd expected, but the body of a girl, her skin vanilla-black, her eyes on mine still as a stopped heart. I carried her into the house, she was light as if her limbs were reeds, and I set her on a rocking chair and brewed her a cup of tea but she would not drink it. She refused broth and bread. Only when I gave her a saucer of honey did she put out a slim tongue and lap a little and sip some water as well. Then she curled up and went to sleep.

"She slept so much those first days, I think she must have undergone a traumatic journey before she arrived to sing outside my door. When she was awake I spoke to her but she only stared at me, her eyes enormous within the delicate architecture of her cheekbones. And though I loved to watch her I grew impatient with her stillness, her silence. At first she cowered if I came near, but slowly she seemed to become comfortable with my presence and one morning I woke with her body next to mine, receiving my heat.

"No one had ever taught me how to love. My life had been concerned with seedpods and root hairs and pressed leaves and confronted with a beating heart I was stymied. I approached her as a specimen, holding her down and prodding her body, but she squirmed out of my grasp and dashed through the rooms, finally hiding under my desk, watching me with those great expressionless eyes and trembling. I pulled her out and tried to make her speak, to say my name, but she would not. Would not or could not. I did not know what to do and was terrified she'd escape so I wove the wicker cage you saw in the front burrow and placed her inside. In the cage I placed honey and water but she would not touch them and began to waste, pretty skin dulling, ribs like basketry, eyes bigger and brighter than ever. 'Only say my name,' I told her, 'only say my name and I'll release you,' but she was silent.

"At last toward dawn one night I heard a few notes, so softly, so disconsolately uttered, their paucity heartbreaking, and I rushed into the room and lighting a lamp thought at first the cage was empty but then saw on the rattan floor the form I'd first thought to find when I set a trap beneath a tree, the spindle of a nightingale. She was dead.

"This stone marks her grave." The rabbit placed a paw on the granite. "I keep the cage to remind me of my folly, the folly of trying to capture a song, the folly of falling in love."

The rabbit took off his spectacles and buffed them on the fur of his wrist. A long time he said nothing, bent to his spectacles as if absorbed in their polishing, then suddenly flung his arms forward and buried his face in his lap, wailing.

Pico knelt beside him stroking the soft fur of his neck, stroking his ears.

"Please, Master Rabbit," he said, "please don't sob so."

"I am sorry." The rabbit raised his head. "I have lived so long with this story."

"Perhaps another nightingale will happen by," Pico said hopefully.

"I have not heard a song like hers before or since, nor do I expect to."

"At least you can remember it, you can sit by her grave."

"Yes. What else can I do?" The rabbit stared bleakly into the sky, then turned to Pico. "Will you . . . will you stay with me, young traveler? I am lonely and you are pleasant company."

For a moment Pico considered abandoning his journey, staying in the burrow with the rabbit. It would be a quiet life, with its own comforts, much like his life in the library. But he shook his head sadly. "I too am in the grips of the folly of love," he said. "Your story has only hardened my resolve to achieve the conclusion of my own story, and I must be off." He stood up.

"This minute?"

"There is no time to lose." At this the rabbit threw himself at Pico's feet and seized his ankles. "Stay with me," he wailed, "stay with me." Then just as abruptly he stood and brushed himself off, adjusting his spectacles. "No," he said. "No, I will not hold you. I held my bird and she died, I will not hold you."

Footprints are seeds, are words, each kernel rooting, branching to another or dying where it lies. The paths we've trodden are sown furrows and who knows the gardens, forests, fields sprung behind us which we may enter years hence and never recognize as work of our own spawning. See the seed flung wide across the waiting loam, across the sand of a beach. And each footprint the child of its predecessor, with a freedom of direction but not of place, unable to erase what has come before, of infinite influence on what will follow. So the story paces on through the forest, across the pages.

Pico walked on for a week, telling and retelling the stories he'd heard so far on his journey. He noticed one day he was breathing harder and realized the land sloped imperceptibly upward and by the next afternoon the geography had begun to buckle around him. He walked over swells, through gentle troughs with brooks squirming at their bases, most slender as his thigh, but others he had to jump across or flounder through, trousers rolled to the knees, boots held aloft.

He made his camps beside these streams, for the small voice of the water was some comfort as he lay reading by firelight and when he opened his notebook to write he found words within its speech.

Five

The Dream Seller

Next Pico came upon one who had been a vendor of dreams.
A night utterly black, a night like a garment cast across the shoulders of the trees, a shawl of indigo wool folding all light within its weave.

Then a scream.

Pico was raked awake by a howl of such abandoned grief he was instantly up and running, buffeted by branches, sent sprawling by tree roots, the cries so compelling that he was sobbing himself by the time he reached a scant heap of embers just aglow. Beside the coals a woman knelt, thin cotton shredded about her, beautiful breasts bleeding from gashes plowed by her own fingernails. Though her face was mussed from weeping he could see she was lovely.

"Don't cry," he told her, "don't cry," and she began to pummel his chest. He caught her fists and held her while she thrashed and then collapsed against him panting. He sat with her till she shivered in the early chill and then put his jacket and his arms around her and recited all the poems he had by heart. How strange it was to hold a woman again.

At dawn he fetched his knapsack from his own campsite. He smoothed his groundsheet beneath a bush and laid her down and covered her with the blanket and sat by all morning reading from his book of stories while she slept. He tried to lip-read the conversations of her sleep, they seemed so heartfelt, her skin flushed, her pulse throbbing in her neck.

Dreams are the soul of the imagination, the slender and evasive revenants of the shells we erect as our dwellings. We build our shells from the sand of our ground bones, mortared with our very blood, and imagine we fence the dreams away but we only fence them in. A few, the rare, the beautiful, remain as near to the heat of their dreams as children, and we know them by their laughter, by the ease with which they are moved to tears, by our own desire to be around them.

When at last the woman opened her eyes in late afternoon she wept again and Pico did not know if it was from the sorrow of her dreams or the sorrow of waking.

"Don't cry," he said, "don't cry," and she quieted and watched him while he dampened a handkerchief at the mouth of his canister and dabbed at the blood that stained her breasts and hands. He handed her his comb and one of his shirts, then took up bow and quiver and went off in search of game.

When he returned an hour later with a dressed rabbit, a handful of wild garlic and a sprig of thyme, she wore the shirt and had carded her hair into a cloudy curlicue at the nape, a transformation from lunatic to belle. Her eyes, long and heavy-lidded, followed his movements. Her lips so full as to seem bruised. As he built up the fire Pico chattered about his library in the city by the sea, about his favorite books, those he'd read over and over so he knew just the lurch his heart would make when he turned the page and encountered the illustration of the despondent dragon under a half-moon or the fervor with which he flipped the final pages of another, the story so vivid he felt his relationship with that book was less an act of reading than a visit, a place he went to. None he'd met on his journey through the forest had read stories but he always longed to talk about books, and so to stave off the smouldering stare of this strange woman he indulged that yearning.

He jointed the rabbit and stewed it with the thyme, adding the garlic toward the end so as not to lose the pungency, further seasoning it from his boxes of salt and pepper. Then they ate with their fingers, sucking the marrow, taking turns swilling pot liquor.

All through the meal and as night fell she said not a word and he wondered if madness had stolen her speech, but decided she was simply returning to the world of human company after days or weeks or months of private sorrows. He as well, encountering others after long spells of solitude, found that words did not surface readily from his throat.

After supper he laid branches on the fire, opened his book and propped his head on his hand to read but could not concentrate under the somber eyes of his companion and so began to read aloud:

"Once, at the edge of an endless sea, in a shack of whale bones shingled in sharkskin, a fisherman lived with his five daughters and one son. Each day he rose an hour before dawn and shoved his dory into the waves, casting his nets to left and right and if he was lucky returned at dusk with fish enough to feed his family and if not they supped on cold kelp soup.

"His hope had been that his son would learn the fishing trade but the boy grew into an indolent youth, given to midmorning risings and siestas that stole half the afternoons. Though his sisters pinched and shouted, though they clobbered him with driftwood, he could not wake in time to fish with his father and would smile sheepishly, curling up to sleep on a swath of sun-warmed sand, his calico cat droning against his belly, shells and the stippled blown eggs of sea urchin carapaces by his ears like faulty receptacles for his dreams.

"He loved to dream, waking to the salty fish stews or seaweed soups and the sting of his sisters' briny tongues as little as possible, always eager to return to the inner tides of the imagination.

" 'Where do the dreams go when I wake up?' he'd asked his mother. 'I've looked in the shells but they're empty.' And she'd taken him outside and sat him on her knee and shown him the stars.

" 'Beyond the stars you see are other stars, stars beyond stars,' she told him, 'and all are dreams, like shoals of fish in the oceans of the night.'

" 'How can I go there?' he asked but she didn't know and soon afterward she died, worn out with childbearing and lack of love.

"After her death he asked his sisters about their dreams but they scoffed and told him that only children dream, that they'd stopped dreaming years ago.

" 'Why do you sleep, then?' he asked.

"'To get strength to work the next day,' they replied. 'Some of us do work, you know,' and they began again to berate him for his laziness but he closed his eyes and his breathing eased into the seesaw sighs of snores.

"'Why don't you sail into the sky and look for your dreams?' he asked his father another day as the weary man mended nets but the fisherman told his son the world was round.

"One evening the fisherman failed to return from the sea. Next morning the upturned dory lay a little way down the beach, brought in by the tide, followed three days later by the body of the fisherman, fat for once, eyes eaten by crabs. The sisters buried him in a shallow grave above the tide line and then, realizing they'd starve alone in the whale-bone shack, set off to seek suitors, fortunes or at least food. They ordered, then pleaded with their brother to join them but he shook his head.

"'You'll die here, then,' they said. 'You don't know how to fish and if you did you wouldn't know how to cook them. You can't even light a fire.'

"He shrugged and rucked the fur of his cat's neck and finally they left. He went to sleep as soon as they'd gone, waking in the middle of the night and walking outside into a sky whose stars hung so low he felt he strolled among them and he could see indeed, so clear the air, the very flames of their inner workings.

"At the strand's edge he looked out to the horizon and saw where the water ended, where one might sail on into the ether.

"He walked to where the boat lay like a turtleback on the sand and with much effort righted it. The mast had snapped but he stepped a whale rib ripped from the rafters of the hovel in its place, lashed another crossways and to the bone beam bound a bedspread, a patchwork counterpane for a sail.

"The cat jumped in and he lugged the boat into the waves and set about steering the craft as the sail belled to the curve of the world. The rocking of the boat was like the rocking of a cradle and he fell asleep at the tiller and woke, hours or weeks later, feeling marvelously awake. The cat perched in the prow like a figurehead, mewing when the spray wet its whiskers, and the young man could see he neared his destination for just beyond the cat's cantilevered ears the sea ended. He held the gunwales as the boat slipped the clutches of the waves but the transition was seamless. He didn't look back to see what became of the water, for his eyes were intent on the hot creatures he moved among, their evanescent stares, their fiery crests, their hissed salutations. In the triangular cubbyhole beneath the stern he found his father's nets. He pulled them out and untangled them and cast them into the deeps of the sky, left and right, fishing for dreams."

As Pico ended his story the woman looked up from her hands and said in a voice gritty from disuse but resonant, a flawed bell, "I too am in love with dreams."

"Have you come to this forest as I have, seeking them?" Pico asked gently.

"Seeking them or fleeing them, I no longer know."

"You have been here long?"

"Yes. No. Dream time is not the sun's time or the moon's time."

"Have you been asleep?"

"Asleep, awake. I don't know, I don't know." She touched each eyelid with a finger as if to verify her waking state. "Touch me," she said so he took her hand and held it, warm and soft as a bird nestling in his lap.

"My name is Pico. Tell me your name."

"Zelzala, they called me," she said after a moment. "I was a vendor of dreams."

"You sold dreams?"

"From a table by the side of the boulevard. Yes." She was silent again, moving the fingers of her free hand across her flushed face, lightly across her breasts.

"Tell me," she said wearily, as though her memories were a weight. "You tell stories. Tell me about yourself."

So Pico told her of the city by the sea and his library and love of a winged girl there and of his vision of the morning town. He told at length of his journey through the forest and the beings he'd encountered for she listened with a somber intensity, inhaling his words through her eyes, such a burning within them he wondered that her lids had not seared away.

He talked at length, and when he'd finished telling of his time in Master Rabbit's house and his last days traveling to this valley she sighed and mumbled "Thank you" and lay down to sleep again.

She slept so much he only gleaned her story in fragments which he ordered in his mind while she slumbered. A story told like a remembered dream, flotsam of a shipwreck bobbing to the surface, gathered on the shore and pieced into a makeshift skiff.

In some city, some nameless city of nights, she set a table under trees at the side of a boulevard where others called their wares. Smouldereyed, she sat in the shadows beside a table laid with a violet cloth. On the cloth burned a fire, a fire that required no fuel, that consumed no oxygen, for it was a flame manufactured from the imaginations of passersby. Yet the breezes swayed it, yet it cast its light.

Men and women came to her. Children. She set her table under the boughs after midnight and they came, the sleepwalkers and insomniacs, the deranged, the lovelorn. The lonely. They knelt before her on the flagstones and she looked into their eyes, her palms together, looked a long age into their souls, then pulled apart her hands and, lo, between them in a glittering window opened onto the night gleamed her wares, the dreams of those who came to her. No, it was not her dreams she hawked but those of the multitudes, she retrieved and offered them the dreams lost inside their own skulls. They chose one or two of the bright images which she plucked forth and whispered back into their ears. Her clients paid then and returned to their beds, to sheets reeking of solitude, to dream a dream of their own devising, called into being by the woman who was the vendor of dreams.

Before dawn she folded her violet cloth and the fire within it, folded the table and stool, and descended to her cellar room. Half the room was taken up by an enormous bed channeled by her hips and shoulder blades, scattered with pillows of the tenderest eiderdown, rumpled silk sheets and cotton blankets. The high windows were draped in velvet so the noon sun soaked in as a bloody taint. There she'd light a stick of sandalwood, change the nightgown she wore for another from her array, for indoors or out she only wore nightgowns, and sink into the bed, drowning in feathers and fabulous dreams. Not her own dreams. She dreamed the dreams of her customers, choosing according to her mood. Sometimes she'd want the dream in which she suckled a kitten at her breast, some days the dream of the falling tree with fruit like eyes, or the one of the singing stones. The dream of the slow boat on the river of blood or the underground cavern where she rode the transparent fish, the one where her flesh sloughed away and she climbed a cliff bone naked to the place where grew a flower on fire. The dream about the naked children playing tambourines on a hillside. The dream about the city of huge women. Other dreams. Dreams even more eccentric, the plots leaping erratic as locusts. And so her room filled with voices, she could hear them when she entered, could see the subtle buckling of the air where the dreams knocked against the surface of this world. She knew them and would call them to her, these favorite reveries she kept about her, her friends.

She rose in the evenings and mounted the steps to the street and wandered on the boulevard buying tidbits from snack sellers. Roasted chestnuts, salted peanuts, mushroom pastries, cherry tarts, candies made of milk and almonds. She ate less for nourishment than comfort, for she attended elaborate feasts in her dreams, candlelit meals for two on barren moors, banquets on pleasure rafts serenaded by lute-playing larks.

In her nightgown she walked the streets, a barren somnambulist, eyes averted from those of the passersby. Even the children would not run after her, even young men, though stirred by the sway of her breasts beneath the thin cotton, would not catcall, for all knew her as the vendor of dreams, Zelzala, she who lived apart.

One night a man she'd never seen before came to her, a tall man with black hair braided down his back, a tapering goatee and eyes that sucked all the fire off her table. He wore black trousers tucked into tall black riding boots, a white shirt pleated at the wrists and an emerald scarf about his throat. A silver chain lay on his chest. He pulled a pouch fashioned from a bull's scrotum from his pocket and tipped a gold hillock onto the table.

"Show me my dreams," he said, kneeling before her, hands at his breast like a supplicant, and she felt a sudden pang, an emotion in her belly she fumbled at before realizing it was desire, something she'd never felt before outside her dreams. Here was danger, she knew, but could not pull away. And so she raised her head and descended into his soul. How patiently he knelt there while she delved, excavating this mine, following lines of silver lode down the loops of his arteries to the apartments of his heart, the four chambers curtained in red velvet. "A heart like a bonfire," she said, "to consume you, and you wish to be consumed. When I entered I was unsure I could stay and still exist but when I left with a handful of dreams and arrived back in my body the dawn was almost upon us."

"Quick," she said, parting her palms. "Choose your dream." But she had slipped in with those gathered from his heart one of her own devising in which she stood naked before him, hands lifting her breasts like offerings of ripe fruit, lips parted to reveal a hint of heat within and he smiled and pointed and she whispered herself into his ear.

That day he carried her body away to his sleep and she carried his to her dark room, her soft bed. She flung herself upon the blankets without even changing her nightgown or lighting the incense and found herself within the throes of his body. Five nights, five days she did not leave her bed, moving through all the dreams she had stolen from the tall stranger, and when she woke she knew the spell was broken. She must leave her existence of figments and enter the light of the sun. From her elective hibernation she walked up four steps and opened her door to a morning so bright, so full of clamor and haste she stood still an hour simply to allow her eyes to adjust while old dreams swirled past her through the door she'd left ajar and evaporated in the starless sky. Her pupils unused to the constriction required so at first the street seemed a river of ghosts on fire. Trees torrents of stars. But slowly she emerged from her long nighttime and was able to look around and accept the colors and commotion into herself and then take a step. That day more alien to her than any dream she'd encountered.

All through the city she asked for him, describing his long hair the color of serpents, his tall boots and emerald scarf, describing the effect of his eyes on her heart, and she was shunted from quarter to quarter, sent down alleys and up hills, knocking on this door and that, for all had heard rumor of this tall man. She met those kind and unkind, the helpful and the indifferent, the soothing and the lewd, and at last encountered an old woman sitting beneath a persimmon tree on the outskirts of the city. She told her tale, describing the stranger she sought, and the woman nodded with no surprise and smiled sadly.

"Go back," she said, "go back to your bed and your nocturnal vocation, abandon this pursuit."

"I cannot. He has consumed my mind. His body has destroyed my dreams."

"Then," said the old woman, "no words of mine may turn you back. You must enter the forest," and she pointed to the green dusk far below. "For you have been loved by a demon. He comes at night to lick and enter the bodies of young women as they sleep and returns to his sylvan abode by day. Many are the girls who have left their lamplit rooms in their nightgowns and walked into the forest seeking that vanished lover, and none has ever returned. Go now, go and do not look back," and the crone prodded Zelzala's side with a hand like a brush broom and she set off down the long slope into the forest.

How long she had wandered here she did not know, and she did not know either the direction of her home. All she had left, now that she had rent her nightgown in her despair, were the dreams of her demon lover that would not fade.

"Have you seen him?" she pleaded. "Have you heard rumor of him, has his voice come to you on any wind?" but Pico shook his head.

"I'm sorry," he said.

"Ah, never mind. I will sleep again. He is there, in my dreams." And she lay down beside the remains of the fire and her breathing instantly slowed.

Three nights and days he stayed with her, cooking for her and eking from her the story, tucking the blanket around her while she slept and watching her face while she dreamed.

"I must move on," she said on the third evening. "Deeper into the forest. But you have fed me and held me and heard my story. Would you like to dream?"

"I have no money to pay."

"Look at me."

So he did, and felt a curious sensation within himself as though gentle feelers, the antennae of silverfish or the whiskers of tiny mice, probed the crannies of his body, a sweeping, a dusting of the nerve ends. After a long time she blinked slowly and smiled and opened her hands. "Choose," she told him.

He saw in a pod of light between her palms like bright seeds his dreams.

He read a book made of lightning. He stole a cupful of sea breeze. He wore horns and danced by a fire. He searched a cave for fallen words. He leaped winged with a golden girl from the seashore.

To this last he gestured of course, to the dream of flying, and she closed his eyes with her fingertips, said "Sleep, sleep," and the end of her exhortation was lost in the aurora of the dream she'd plucked from him and handed back.

Before them is the sea so blue, the sun laying a street with cobbles of gold, and the waves are at his feet. He takes her hand and they lift together from the stamped sand, and about them now is the maelstrom of their wings' motion like their own brilliant and antic shadows. The sun hot as a new-minted coin on his cheeks, the waves furling, slapping up brine. The gulls that have followed them, elbowing each other like unruly bridesmaids, now curl back to shore and the lovers leave the wet wind above the sea and pull into the sky, into the sun-beaten blue that deepens as they ascend. Here the air will hold them and they ride it like a carpet, both hands joined now, and he looks into her face. The face he knows better than his own and is yet so foreign his heart hurts at each new glance. The face that is life buoy and talisman, noose, shelter and shackle. They come together to kiss, the swiveling sun, the indigo sky, the shriveling sea, the whole world heaved into their lips, and he opens his eyes again and she is laughing.

He woke with her laughter upon him and a feeling like the morning after the first night you know she loves you. "Oh," he said. Feeling so full he thought he'd shatter into a thousand triangles of sunlight. "Oh, oh."

Zelzala had gone. She'd left behind the remnants of her cotton nightgown, the remnants of a beautiful dream. Pico, glad as a frog after the rain, packed up his camp, shouldered his knapsack and sang as he swung on his way. And he knew she'd given him a gift perhaps greater than any other received on his travels. The gift of his own desire, to sustain him.

The air cooled as he walked on across the rising land and now when he slept he wrapped himself around the fire as though it were a hot child he sheltered and he woke once or twice each night to lay on branches. The canopy was again low as it was at the outset of his journey, the ground wetter underfoot. An abundance of mushrooms.

Then abruptly he was among pines, their voices sibilant after the raucous deciduous trees he'd left. Their scent cool as steel. He walked on the fragrant pallets of their needles along jagged avenues for two days, moving up long ridges. In the afternoon of the second day he heard splashing and came upon a waterfall churning into a small green pool. He took off his clothes and walked into the pool across rocks vivid with moss and he drank the water that tasted of rust and resin and let the cataract break across his back, his shouts echoing. He slept that night in the company of the waterfall and there he had another dream.

A beautiful woman wearing nothing but a faded blue work shirt walks up to the door of a house in a forest and knocks. A tall man opens it, black hair about his shoulders, and he leans and kisses her lips and takes her hand and leads her into the house. They pass through empty room after empty room, the only furniture the angled pillars of dust they set aswarm with their passage. All the rooms are identical and it seems they are moving endlessly into and out of the same room until at last they arrive at a room from which there is no exit save by the way they came in. In the middle of this room stands a bed with a single white sheet upon it, luminous in the light of early morning. The tall man turns to her and unbuttons the shirt she wears, slowly, as if each buttonhole is a door to yet another room, and when she is naked he lays her on the bed. Loosing the emerald scarf from his neck he tears it into four ribbons and binds her wrists and ankles to the bedposts. Then he begins to undress.

And whether this was a dream of hers, a fantasy slipped into his ear along with his own dream or whether he had somehow visioned her encounter at last with her demon lover he did not know. But he believed the latter. He believed the beautiful vendor of dreams had left her world of nights and intangibles and come at last to a house of touch from which there would be no escape, no escape from ecstasy.

Six

The City in the Mountains

B y midmorning next day Pico had walked through the last of the
pines and into fields of strawberries. Before him, their peaks too
bright to look at, a mountain range reared across a third of the sky. He
stood on a plateau at the base of the mountains, planted with gardens
and orchards, and in the elbow between the slopes and the cultivated
land, directly before him and a little above, was a city, close-packed
houses, streets petering up into the rocks, the walls of dark stone
pocked with darker windows. And the thought of that abundance of
people after his lonely days was breathtaking. Above the city a solitary
scar of a trail swayed up through stone to a clot between two peaks, a
scab in the white, its form uncertain at this distance, it could have
been a rockslide or wall or house that drew the eye, tantalizing and
somehow grim.

So the thin-shouldered poet, battered hat on his head, battered
pack on his back, walked through fields of strawberries, fields of

rhubarb, among apple trees and peach trees, to the city in the mountains. He passed farmers in the fields and farmers pushing carts laden with potatoes and turnips and pumpkins and he doffed his hat and greeted them and they nodded in reply and one tossed him a green-skinned apple. Slowly he walked this last stretch, savoring the light and space, the scents of fruit blossom and scythed grass, the sour juicy apple. A tawny interlude between the darkness he'd emerged from and the streets of the city before him.

In early afternoon he was past the fields and climbing on a rutted track littered with crushed fruit, loud with bees. A smattering of cloud had begun to spume off the tops of the mountains and as he neared the houses and the track turned to stone the sky filled and he entered the halls of the city through the curtains of a soft drizzle.

The streets of the city in the mountains were narrow, cobbled with rounded river stones, and they twisted with little respite, adjusting to the convoluted landscape so one was always climbing or descending, sometimes so steeply the street was a staircase hacked into bare rock. A great torrent between high bolstered banks churned through the city's center, the milky water spanned by a hundred bridges of varying shape and size, from planks with rope banisters to a great arch thronged with statues from whose apex every roof might be seen.

All that afternoon Pico walked the streets in the rain between walls of carven stone with their jealous windows. He passed the people of the city who strode swiftly and wore long coats of blue or black wool against the chill, scarves about their throats, and all held umbrellas aloft. They did not notice this meager stranger in their midst, though he moved in a slower rhythm, though he peered into their faces, into their windows, and if a door was opened craned to glimpse a carpeted hallway, a lamplit interior.

He came upon a street of shops and stopped before a bakery, breaths of fragrant steam exhaled each time a customer opened the door. Behind the window were cinnamon rolls and herb loaves and glazed donuts, and deeper within he could see the yellow of the oven mouth. He stopped short after a moment, backing into the path of a passerby, for in the mirror of the steamed glass he had seen and recognized the stranger who was himself. Hard edges to his cheeks now, a novel sturdiness in his gaze, a rigidity to his spine. His hair long, tied with twine away from gold-hooped earlobes. He pushed up his sleeve to look at the tattoo of the iris on his arm. The journey through the forest marked on his skin as his footprints had marked the skin of the forest. The words of the forest inside him as he had left words behind. A long time he stood before the glass, turning this way and that, trying to enter the new body before him, this body of scars and angles, this foreigner.

He walked slowly on, the hunger grinding his bowels overridden by the eagerness to explore, until he came to the city's central boulevard, which wound like a long park perpendicular to the river, along which mothers pushed infants in hooded carriages, earnest young men leaned together gesturing, girls flitted and swayed flinging giggles and glances wantonly as though they strewed petals. And also the solitary walked here, looking into the distance as though disdainful of what was near. But all were young. There were no old men nodding on benches, no old women cackling over babies.

Already waiters were setting ironwork tables out under the trees, bearing armfuls of linen, cutlery, crockery, paring wax from the sockets of candlesticks. In late afternoon the sky cleared to a more vivid blue than Pico had seen save in dreams. It was the blue Sisi had spoken of, blue of the upper sky. Later came other blues. The blues of evening. Blue of cigarette smoke, blue of pent blood, of moonlight through a wave, blue of a cold nipple, a bruised eye. He imagined he inhaled the blue air like hashish for his mind skimmed like a skipped stone, tapping the cobbles, the restaurant facades, the shadows beneath the trees, the parade of faces, then lifting again into haze. He reached the end of the boulevard, turned and walked back toward the bridge through growing crowds among the tortures of fresh coffee and frying bean cakes, strawberry crepes and rhubarb tarts, for the snack sellers had lit their charcoal stoves and crouched over foaming oil or frying pans, folding their wares into paper cones and receiving the clink of coins into their palms.

Fire-eaters gushed hot bushes over the heads of the crowd, spraddle-legged sword-swallowers sucked steel, a boy mounted a ladder balanced on the soles of a prone man, handstanding on the topmost rung. A man tore coins with his fingers, another passed coins through the ears of children. And Pico knew that it was here, in the deepest shadows beneath the trees, that Zelzala had unfolded her table with its violet cloth, before a stranger lured her to the forest by the ardor of his heart.

From pool to pool of fragrant warmth he walked, steaming the damp from his clothes at successive braziers. Only when halfway up the great arched bridge did he realize he was above water and he moved to the stone balustrade and leaned looking over the city that lay like a plague of fireflies against the mountains. After a while he placed his knapsack against the ankle of one of the giant statues that stood at intervals along the bridge and sat on the balustrade with his back to the pack, smoking the stub of his last cigarette. And suddenly he was more lonely than he had ever been in his travels. Even the solitary walkers had homes to go to, a sister or an uncle to drink a cup of coffee with. Those he'd met in the forest had also been lonely but here, surrounded by laughter and camaraderie, he craved companionship so sorely it sucked the energy from his bones. He could hardly lift the cigarette to his lips.

Later the river of people thinned so the voice of the other river rose louder to his ears. The windows began to wink out. Laughter from a last few groups at the outdoor tables. He pulled his blanket from his knapsack, tucked it around him and slept.

The cold woke him before dawn, his joints stiff. Outside the cocoon of the blanket he began to shake so he could hardly pick up the knapsack, kneecaps snapping, jaws rattling. Blanket across his shoulders, he walked down to the boulevard while the sky grayed above the mountains. A few street sweepers were already shoving oily paper and soggy crusts into gutters and he walked ahead of them searching for something, anything, to eat but the scraps of food were trodden and damp. Sifting a heap of paper cones he heard a tinkle and uncovered a single small coin fallen into the crack between cobblestones. Feverishly he hunted for more but found only peach pits, walnut shells, cockroaches.

When the first waiters began to unlock the doors and right the chairs which had been placed upside down on tabletops he chose a cafe on the western side of the boulevard which would receive the first light as the sun breasted the mountains. A waiter came over rubbing his eyes, smacked the tabletop with a rag, and smoothed a checked cloth over it. Pico placed his coin on the cloth.

"Good morning. I'm new to this city. What will this coin buy me, please?"

The waiter tugged the rag between his fists and cocked an eyebrow. "I beg your pardon, sir, but did you say you're new in the city?"

"I arrived yesterday after some months traveling. I come from the city by the sea on the western edge of the forest."

The waiter frowned a moment then chortled. "A bottle too many last evening, sir?"

Pico stared at him then shrugged, too weary to argue. "Can I get some sort of breakfast with this coin?"

The waiter picked up the gold disc. "What will you have?"

"Coffee. Do you have pastries?"

"Apricot, cheese."

"Bring me as many of each as this coin will buy, please."

He took out a book and tried to read but was too light-headed to concentrate. He stared bleakly at the paling peaks till the waiter returned with a blue mug of coffee, blue bowls of milk and sugar and a plate of amber half-moons. The first mouthful of cheese pastry almost sent him into a swoon. He wolfed another and another then realized his stomach could not take any more, so long had he been hungry. So he cradled the coffee mug, breathed the steam into his face and watched the seeping dawn.

Slowly the tables around him filled with early risers who glanced at the sky and clutched their umbrellas. They ordered coffee and pastries as he had or more elaborate platters of omelets and beans and white cheese, and to Pico's astonishment and delight a woman at the next table pulled a book from a reticule and began to read. He leaned to peer at the spine but the title and author were unknown to him. The woman, noticing his attention, pouted and swiveled slightly away. Embarrassed, Pico bent to his coffee.

Later that morning he spied others reading on park benches or glimpsed them reading on sofas behind windows with steaming drinks at their sides and at noon the alley he wandered opened into a square with a sculpture of a reading man at its center. All around the square great wardrobes sagging with books stood under huge dark parasols that drooped like decaying leaves and the booksellers sat beside their wares on folding chairs reading or scribbling with pencil or pen into notebooks large or small. A few customers tipped down volumes and leafed through them, sampling sentences.

With a sense of fulfilment stronger even than the sating of his hunger that morning, for he'd been starved of books much longer than of food, Pico joined the browsers. Inhaling the odor of mildewed hide as if he'd entered a confectionery, fondling the bindings of stippled leather or buckled cloth, running his fingers across the raised letters of the titles as though blind, for a moment he wished he'd saved the coin to buy a book, then giggled at his folly.

He'd not heard of any of the authors. He read the first pages, looked at chapter headings, at the illustrations under their sheets of filmy paper. It began to rain, an abrupt applause on the umbrellas, and he took a book and crouched in the lee of a wardrobe, the owner of which was scribbling oblivious to all else, and read a story. And knew even as he read that he'd remember every word, would hold in his memory the sensation of crouching on cold cobbles while the rain sprayed mist against his cheeks, reading a new story in a strange city. He stood and looked into the square where a few figures under umbrellas scurried like black beetles, where the rain flung fleeting tin crowns on the stones, where a stone man endlessly pored over pages that would not perforate under rain or sun, reading the first book and the last, book of winds, book of light.

The scribbling bookseller looked up.

"Forgot your umbrella?"

"I don't have an umbrella."

The bookseller nodded as if this were a symptom of some quirky illness. He gestured toward the books. "Looking for a particular work?"

"No. Just browsing, if that is permitted."

"Please," he gestured expansively.

"Where do the books come from, if I may ask?"

"They're all secondhand. I haunt auctions and wheedle my way into attics and those moving house tote me cartons of tomes that have cluttered shelves unread for years."

"But where are they written? Do they come from other cities?"

"Other cities? What other cities?"

"Are there no other cities near here?"

"This is the city. There is only one, unless you trust in fairy tales. The books are written here, read here."

"And everyone knows how to read?"

"Of course. What cave are you emerging from?"

Pico sighed and shook his head. "The forest. I arrived yesterday from the forest."

The bookseller smiled rather warily, said "Take your time" and bent again to his notebook.

All that afternoon it rained and he moved around the square from dripping parasol to parasol partaking of the books written in the city, which were full of the cobbled streets and the boulevard and the hundred bridges and the shifting carapace of umbrellas and the incessant rain and the sad musicians. The stories had something of the claustrophobia of those dense alleys, the endless diversions interspersed with warm interiors. He began to know a little of the hearts of these city folk, their pent emotions, their reverence for duels, suicides, fraught love triangles. At the edges of the tales he glimpsed the white peaks of the mountains and the dark fringes of the forest but these were never penetrated. They hung like ponderous ornaments on the fabric of the prose, mute and meaningful. And he sensed something else beneath the tales, some force that gave them power, evident in fearful glances and unheard murmurs, in the absence of certain words, in the avidity for unnatural death. Melancholy processions, rites rich with hidden meaning, girls curdling suddenly mad, a road, untraveled, curving away from the city to an untold destination.

What he did know as the rain died to a drizzle at evening was that he would have to stay awhile in this city learning to wear the new face the forest had given him, learning this new literature.

.   .   .

A city of squalls, foggy mornings, intervals of blue and white so immaculate the eyes ached. A city of readers, coffee drinkers, kissers on sidewalks, sad faces at wet windows. A city of umbrellas, woolen scarves, raincoats, cigarettes, wineglasses, cognac.

Pining, Pico wandered several days at its edges among the faces of strangers, living off crumbs, crusts and bruised fruit, craving coffee and nicotine, craving company, seeking an entrance to the lives of its people. But those he approached regarded him as mildly lunatic when he began to relate his tale.

By the evening of his fourth day, stomach clenched, clothes perpetually damp, he was wandering on the steeper streets of the quarter where the houses leaned like drunken comrades, where the refuse lay sopping in nooks and the interiors harbored dingy dimness. Dogs bickered over bones and dirty urchins gripped his coat and he put their hands into his pockets and apologized for not being able to help. Sots regarded him balefully over the lips of wine bottles.

He was running a light fever like a glaze of flame over his skin, making all shapes vivid. Arriving at the last houses he looked along the dark scar that continued up among the rocks till it was lost in shadow. The road he would have to take one day but not yet, not yet. He would not survive in the mountains without provisions and knew he couldn't continue his journey without respite. He'd have to leave the city though, he thought, and descend into the fields and orchards where he could filch fruit and vegetables at night. But the idea of retracing his steps was a lime seed in his mouth. He sat on a cold stone, the city a twinkling bed of mica below, its voices rising like the speech of a whisperer and he strove to hear its secret word, the word the city was saying over and over. He would have to learn the word this city was keeping under its breath.

Unbattened, the wind whipped chill on the bare mountainside, moaning between leaning stones, so he stood and walked again. He entered an alley which he realized after a few steps was a cul-de-sac ending in a reeking midden and he turned to exit, slipped on some foul patch of swill and landed against a wall, hips in a gutter. This position of repose seemed more attractive than trudging aimlessly though forsaken streets and he adjusted his pack beneath him and closed his eyes, not budging even when a rat squatted a moment on his torso to preen its face.

A minute or an hour later he heard a girl crying and thought it was Sisi and then Adevi and then a gruff voice muttered and he was awake. Silhouetted against the aperture of the cul-de-sac two figures leaned against a wall, the form of a girl cowering in the gutter and that of a man propped against the wall with one hand, the other swinging at intervals into the girl's face.

Pico struggled out of the straps of his knapsack and stumbled toward the pair. "Excuse me," he said. The man stopped swinging and turned toward him with a grunt. The girl whimpered. "Please stop hitting her," Pico said. "You're making her cry."

The man grunted again and resumed smacking the girl so Pico stepped up, tapped his shoulder, then thrust his fist hard as he could into the man's face. He felt the crunch of bone and did not know if it had come from his hand or the man's head. He assumed the man would come after him but to his surprise the brute reeled on the cobbles clutching his nose, then staggered off around a corner. The girl had slumped to the ground. She shuddered when he reached out a hand. "It's all right," he said. "I won't hurt you."

Black in the meager light a tendril of blood traced the curve of her cheekbone from a cut above her eyelid. Stark prints of four fingers reddened her neck. Already her cheeks and eyes were swollen. He fetched his knapsack and took out the water bottle and wet a hand-kerchief and dabbed at the blood. "It will be all right now," he said. He could see the glitter as her eyes lifted to his face.

"Can you stand?"

She nodded.

"Here." He took her hands and with a visible mustering of grace she pulled herself to her feet, leaned on his arm. He picked up the pack.

"I'll walk with you a little way. Till you get your strength."

They moved out of the dead-end street and the girl motioned to the left and they began to walk, carefully as though the cobblestones were treacherous, not speaking, not looking at each other, holding on tightly.

Before they reached the end of that street they heard a shout, clattering footsteps. Slowly they turned to face the four men who descended on them, one the girl's assailant, the lower half of his face a beard of blood, the other three black-capped, bearing bludgeons. Pico stepped in front of the girl and held up a hand. "Stop," he said but the wallop of a club on his ear shoved him abruptly into the dark.

Far above like a square scored moon four vertical blue ribbons hovered in the darkness. His head was a drum beaten by a maniac, tongue a board against his palate. Something felt cold on his ankle. As he reached down to touch a metal band he realized his hand was so swollen the fingers would not straighten. The band was soldered closed, attached to a chain, and he followed the chain to a great iron globe, then withdrew his hand. He closed his eyes, retreating into dreams that seemed to move much faster than normal.

Later a clang and an iron door scrabbled open, a lamp held in a great fist illuminating the tall stone box he lay in. The jailor, shaven-headed, in a short black robe, set a tin bowl and cup on the stone floor within Pico's reach and exited. Water, a lentil gruel. He sipped the water slowly and after a while was able to sup the lentils, the first hot food he'd had in a week. So this is how it ends, he thought. A dungeon in a strange land, friendless. He laughed shortly, a dry cackle like a file on metal, and the sound shuttled around the walls disconcertingly so he did not speak aloud again. Noises reverberated through the door, a gong, distant shrieks, footsteps endlessly advancing, retreating.

That first day in the jail was the worst he'd ever known, worse than the day the old librarian died, worse than the day Sisi left him. At those times the world, however bleak, had sprawled around him. And he'd had books in which to drown himself. But the cage is the ultimate horror.

Time passing was the swelling and fading of light in the barred window, the scrape of the door and clink of the bowl and cup on stone. He tried to keep track of the days but soon lost count. Once he spoke to the jailor but got a boot in the belly so he whispered poems to keep himself company, seizing even on echoing screams as salve for his loneliness. He entered moods of utter desolation, boredom so invidious he became desperate to kill himself. At other times he grew queerly euphoric, a bowl of sour porridge a king's banquet, a poem an orchestra in his mouth. Often in the forest, daunted by the task of foraging for his food, he'd imagined a private room where he no longer had to move, where he could sleep and accept food brought to him, but now that dream had become a nightmare. He would have faced starvation simply to place a foot in free air.

Over and over he conversed with his friends from the forest, asking new questions, imagining their replies. How he'd have loved to hear Balquo's deep voice, Adevi's harsh chatter, Zelzala's drowsy mumbling. Conversations in the flesh are the first drafts toward the later conversations of the mind, where words and ideas are sorted and elaborated, recast.

He was asleep when the door banged open in a clutter of sparks. The jailor placed a lamp beside his head, then knelt with chisel and mallet and hammered the band off his ankle. He yanked Pico upright and shoved him toward the door, then led him down the murky passages past moans, past unspeakable reeks. At the top of a long flight of stairs the jailor sorted among keys on a massive ring, unlocked a door and tossed Pico out into the night and the rain.

After the cloistered ammoniac air of the jail the rain was so fresh against his face he simply lay back and let it cover him. But a voice was at his side, a small hand tugged.

"Come. Come with me."

He dragged his eyes to meet the gaze of a girl, the girl he'd helped how many days ago, and now it was she who begged him rise. So he struggled to his feet.

See them walking, the hurt poet and the girl, walking through deserted streets in the rain, supporting each other, moving slowly from pool to pool of lamplight, not speaking. His clothes are torn and threadbare, stained with his own excrement, his boots admit the puddles he steps though, his hat looks like a rotting eggplant. And she. She wears a skirt that twists about her knees, small bells tinkling at its rim. She wears a blue bodice laced low over small breasts, gold-colored slippers, great gold hoops in her ears, brass and green glass bangles up her wrists, a necklace of wooden beads. Her hair dark and loose in the rain.

Now he turns toward her as they enter a spill of light and sees clearly the heartbreaking, heart-shaped face of a girl at the borders of womanhood. A child's skin, child's chin, but eyes older than the face around it, eyes that have done much weeping. And yet there's laughter in the mouth, the mouth like a bruised strawberry. Her face seems to him in his ravaged state a spirit's countenance.

The journey across the city took half the night, so weary was he. At dawn they entered a door and she half dragged him up stairs and into bliss. In a room of perfumes she removed his sopping clothes, sponged warm water over his face from a basin and toweled him dry. Then the rapture of pillows, sheets, blankets, down rather than stone beneath him. Drawn curtains, warmth, sleep.

.   .   .

He woke like a drowned man surfacing, tumbling back, buoyed higher, sinking again, each wave buffeting him closer to daylight, but he stayed as long as he could in this womb of slumber and at the edges of sleep a voice sang words he could not discern.

He opened his eyes at last to a white room. White light fell on the mattress on the floor where he lay, fell on a dressing table backed by a half-moon mirror, tabletop thronged with vials of liquids the colors of pale wines and sunrises, scattered with puffs and paintbrushes, orangewood sticks, picks and files, the implements a woman requires to face the world. Like the cast-off feathers of a molting bird bright garments lay across stools, in gaudy pools on the floor. On the walls were paintings of a naked girl floating among the stars, though she had no wings. Stars circled her head, she danced above trees, above rooftops. And in a green baize armchair beneath drifting curtains the same girl sat mending a blue blouse, quietly singing, and Pico saw her hair, in the light, was the color of poppies.

"Tell me your name," he said.

She looked up and smiled. "You're awake."

"Beautiful one, tell me your name."

"I am Solya."

"My name is Pico. Please, Solya, what are you singing?"

"Listen:

"Overnight the snow has fallen,
a white shroud I welcome.
A thousand eyelids close over me

and naked I sleep, naked I sleep,

waiting till I'm pretty enough

to pull apart my home."

"Ah. What is snow?"

"Snow." She looked at him, then opened the curtains and pointed to the mountains.

"Pico," she said. "A strange name. And what strange clothes you wear. And why don't you know what snow is?"

"If I told you where I come from, Solya, you wouldn't believe me. The people of this city will not accept the story I've lived so long."

"My labor is listening to the stories of sad men. Tell me."

"I'm a stranger in this city. I arrived here some days ago, or weeks, who knows, from a city by the sea on the far side of the forest, where I was once a librarian. I am a poet and a traveler, born of winged parents but wingless. I can throw knives and pick locks. I have sung duets with a minotaur and sipped tea brewed by a rabbit. I am seeking the morning town of Paunpuam, east of the mountains, where I hope to gain my wings."

She put a hand to her cheek then laughed. "I knew," she said. "I knew you were a stranger. Your queer voice which is not like any voice I've heard before and even so seems like a voice I know. But how marvelous. You say you come from a city on the other side of the forest, a city by the . . . by the sea? Tell me, what is the sea?"

"You sang me a song. Listen to a poem, a poem from the far side of the world:

"The sea's utter lust eats at the shores of my skin.

Here at last I can be lonely.

The sky has spilled all its secrets

and the crabs have gathered them to their caves.

The horizon drags my own secrets out with the tide,

out beyond the islands

to where the world tapers.

Here I can believe the world has an end,

that if I swim out far enough

I'll plunge with all the fish across the brink

and fall through thickets of stars.

Even the universe, they say, has walls.

Out beyond the twilight's keeping a door lies open.

I'd like to stand there with my back to all the light,

looking out,

then take a step."

"It's beautiful."

"If only I had my books you could read more but my knapsack was taken from me."

"Your bag. I forgot. He gave me your bag." She pulled Pico's pack from beneath the dressing table and passed it to him. He loosened the drawstring and took out the book of poetry and handed it to her but she did not open it. "I want to hear your voice," she said. "Please tell me more about your city by the sea."

So he began to describe the city he'd left, the spice ships swooping on the waves bearing fragrant cargos from mythic islands, the balconies over the streets, the bare-breasted dancing girls, the flower boxes in every window. He told of the hot afternoons and the bells in the mornings, and as he told of the winged people who rose from the towers at dawn he began to cry.

She set aside the book and her sewing and sat by him on the mattress and took his hand. "What is it?"

"I love a winged girl there, in the city by the sea."

"A winged girl. Does she love you?"

"She did. Once. I am traveling eastward to seek my wings at the morning town of Paunpuam that I might be with her."

Solya clapped her hands. "How lovely. It's all like a story, like something a grandmother might tell. If one had a grandmother. All my life I've heard the forest was endless, that this was the only city in the world. Hearing this from you is like having a visitor from a star."

"Solya. I must ask you. Did you get me out of the prison?"

She shrugged, nodded.

"Why?"

"You came to my aid. Other men would have walked away. Other men have walked away."

"How did you get me out? A bribe?"

She shrugged again and looked out the window.

"Solya. Thank you."

She stood abruptly. "Are you hungry?"

"Famished."

Tossing him a dressing gown she said, "You can put this on. Your clothes are still wet," and he realized he was naked beneath the sheets. As she left the room he saw she walked with a limp but moved so prettily her gait became a dance, deformity co-opted in the service of grace.

She returned with a tray containing two mugs of coffee and a plate of buttered toast and strawberry jam. Pico sat cross-legged on the mattress to eat.

"How lonely you must be so far from home," she said, curling up on the armchair with her coffee.

"I have my memories. But yes, I have been lonely in this city. I've been lonely all my life."

"In this house no one is lonely. Sometimes I long to be alone."

"Is this your parents' house?"

"My parents are dead."

"Oh. I'm so sorry. An orphanage, then?"

"No, not an orphanage. This is a house of sad stories, a house of lipstick and perfumes, a house of secret rooms. The stories are carried here in the heads of men who don't know why they come. Their heads hold all the tears they have not cried since childhood, their skulls would crumble like wet bread if they took off their hats. They pay their gold and walk up the stairs to a room and here they don't know what to do, don't know where they are, don't know what they want. What they want is to tell their sad stories, to wet the sheets not with semen but with tears. They want to hear sweet whispers: 'It will be all right, don't cry, don't cry, big boys don't cry.'"

"So I have come to you with my sad story," said Pico, "and you have accepted my tears as others would not."

"It is my labor."

"I thank you."

Suddenly a knock came at the door and another girl entered. She leaned against a wall, charcoal hair short and straight about a narrow face, and regarded him with a surly stare, then bent to make a cigarette.

"This is Narya," said Solya. Then, as if in explanation, "She's a poet like you."

"Will she let me have a cigarette?" Pico asked and the thin girl tossed him the pouch and papers but did not smile.

Solya had told Narya of her foreign guest and she listened incredulously as he related his story in detail, telling of his aberrant birth and apprenticeship in the library, of the letter he'd found and his journey through the forest studded with the faces of strange and wonderful friends.

Solya asked what the women wore in the city by the sea and he described their cotton dresses, pearl earrings, the cowries they wore in their hair. "But the winged people do not wear clothes," he said. "They choose to let the wind garb them, silks of siroccos, damasked cat's-paws."

"Winged people," Narya muttered. "Is it possible?"

"My mother was winged," he replied.

All that day Solya questioned him about the city by the sea while Narya sat by smoking, watching him with skeptical insolence. He could not help staring at her though, when she hunched over to roll her cigarettes, the cigarettes she took between her lips with such sullen languor, the smoke seeming to surface not from her lungs but her heart. A red-haired girl and a narrow burning girl bewitched by images

carried by a poet through a forest deemed impenetrable. And he likewise asked many things about their city so in the afternoon Solya
sprang up, exclaiming, "Let's walk on the boulevard!"

She found him loose purple pantaloons and a blue sweater and,
giggling, braided his hair. Then the girls bent to the mirror, painting
their faces peacock colors, tulip colors, the colors a slap or bite might
raise on the skin applied as lure. The enticement of violence. Their
clothes garish signposts on the path to breast and buttock.

Through a long hall they led him past doors which whimpered or
moaned as had the doors of the prison, the echos of ecstasy and despair so alike. Down a staircase, out a door, into an alley.

Solya walked with much aplomb, hips and hair careening, eyes
brazenly snagging the gaze of passing men. Narya's allure was less
overt, though her disdainful stare was not less magnetic. Pico felt like
a sparrow on an outing with a pair of parakeets.

They made their supper at the braziers on the boulevard, the girls
haggling shamelessly, paying with coins pulled from purses at their
hips. The bargaining seemed less a symptom of poverty than a desire
for entertainment for they dropped gold into every open violin case
and upturned hat along the way, applauding vigorously and exclaiming at the end of a song or an act. Pico, clutching paper cornucopias
of raspberries and salted peanuts, followed the girls in a daze recalling
the evenings he'd wandered here alone and hungry and his mouth
would not relinquish the smile he'd kept all afternoon.

The girls linked arms and Solya pulled him into the chain and they
sauntered down the center of the boulevard, jostling other parties out
of their way. At first he smiled apologetically and tried to make room

for passersby but his companions barged him through the crowds so he abandoned his timidity and let them sweep him along.

In a tiny garret at the top of the whorehouse Pico made his home. The roof slanted almost to the floor on one side of the room so he could stand upright only along the left-hand wall. A window opened onto a diminutive balcony with a wrought-iron railing, just big enough for a single chair, and there he smoked and sipped coffee, watching the kisses and quarrels on the streets below.

Solya gave him a mattress and he found on a street corner a cane chair lacking a seat that he repaired with twine and he discovered in a gutter a deal table needing only a few nails. A strip of scuffed carpet donated by one of the girls fit nicely on the floor. Against the tall wall he made bookshelves of planks and bricks where he placed the three books he'd carried through the forest. Plenty of space remained for future purchases.

Solya found him work washing dishes in a tiny restaurant run by a woman named Goyra, a dour dwarf with a cough like surf, a cigarette forever wedged in a gap between her lower incisors so one eye was permanently asquint. She stalked the scullery with a whisk to lay on the backs of slack workers or, if her ulcers irked her, on the industrious too. She had a light hand with pastries though, her sauces were subtle, her meat impeccably marinated, and when she bent over the flame Pico devoured her technique, recognizing a fellow artist. He surreptitiously learned the method for a smooth roux, for choux puffs, for frothy mousse, the cooking times for rare lamb and stuffed duckling, the recipe for chocolate cake rich as loam. And the eight tables of her eponymous eatery never held gaps, every evening a queue of salivating elite formed outside the door for she took no reservations. He labored over a tub in the back of the kitchen from dusk till nearly midnight five days a week, plunging plates and pots into scalding suds, piles of porcelain teetering on either side, hands chapping so he had to beg lotion from the girls. But after work he reverently nibbled whatever leftovers he'd managed to scrounge for Goyra, though crotchety, did not grudge her workers scraps.

Girls who are fires. Adevi had been a bonfire, roaring, riotous, ravenous. Get too close and you're a cinder. Zelzala had smouldered like a coal under ashes, like incense-soaked sandalwood. But Solya was a candle flame, clear, bright, steady, a candle flame in a window in rainy weather.

Though she worked at night, Solya flourished in sunshine when the light spelt out the conjugations of orange in her hair, from the yellow of parched grass through colors of fire to the deep amber of old iron.

It was she who nudged Pico through the city those first days, taking him to her favorite cafes, promenading with him along the boulevard in late afternoon before they returned to their workplaces. She bought him an umbrella and, though he protested he knew how to sew, mended his tattered blue velvet coat and ancient hat so deftly the patches were all but indiscernible.

She loved breakfasts, especially if she'd stayed up all night, and she'd bang on his door soon after dawn and drag him off to a cafe where she ordered huge platters of eggs, bacon, sausages, beans, grilled tomatoes. These meals made her garrulous and while Pico nibbled pastries abstemiously she chattered with her mouth full. If Narya came along to drink coffee and smoke the girls bantered about the tricks they'd turned, tabulating in absorbing and hilarious detail this poor man's physical shortcomings, mimicking that man's grunting or the contortions of his features as he climaxed.

He delighted in those breakfasts, the hidden sun heaving light over the mountains, the odor of coffee, the gush of pleasure at the first cigarette of the day. He liked best to see the girls in the mornings, their faces surfacing through the paint, their hair ravaged, ravishing.

One day as he breakfasted alone with Solya a man passed in a gaudy cloak sewn of diamonds of scrap cloth. Gnats of color speckled his trousers, bright crescents clung to his cuticles. A little in front of him as though it were a compass or the ferrule of a cane he held a brown glass bottle by the neck.

"Zarko," Solya called and the man turned, haggard eyes striving to focus on her face, his mouth between a grimace and a grin.

"Will you join us for coffee?" she asked but he waved a hand. "Just had supper. Must get to bed. Must get to . . ." He seemed to discover the bottle and held it up, squinting through the glass, then tipped the dregs into his mouth and flung it into the middle of the street where it burst. He nodded and was about to move on when he noticed Pico. Approaching the table, he seized Pico's head and swiveled it this way and that like a choosy customer examining a melon for blemishes. Pico gripped the tabletop and stared at Solya. At last Zarko released him.

"Who's this?" he demanded.

"Pico," she smiled. "He's a poet and a traveler, a stranger here. He came from the far side of the forest."

"Of course he's a stranger. Look at his eyes. I must own his face. Bring him by this evening."

They watched his labored progress up the boulevard, as he clutched at tables and hollered snatches of song and once sprawled over a sleeping dog, until finally he lurched into an alley. Solya turned back to her breakfast. Her face had grown suddenly old, gaiety snuffed. She raised her eyes to his.

"Who is he?" Pico asked.

"Zarko the painter. My love, my bane."

There in the sidewalk cafe, sipping coffee as the sun sidled across the cobbles and set a match to Solya's hair, he received her story.

She'd been an acrobat, a tightrope walker, loveliest of the entertainers along the boulevard. Between two chestnut trees, high above the cobbles, she'd strung a cord on which she cartwheeled and somersaulted, juggled swords and torches. Her high-wire act became so popular that other performers jigged or trilled or prestidigitated before vacant cobbles, cups and caps empty. Meanwhile the throngs yelped as the red-haired girl sprang and twirled in the sky and when she lowered a basket on a string to reap their coins she had to use both hands to reel it in.

From her precarious perch above the street she'd seen the black-haired man with vivid eyes, he never missed a performance, leaning against a lamppost, sketch pad on his knee, eyes on her body. One evening he approached her and she followed him back to his house where he showed her stacks of sketch pads filled with page upon page of drawings, drawings of her in the air. That night he strung a rope between two beams and bade her remove her clothes and she danced naked on the cord while he painted.

"Ah, the paintings," she sighed. "You've seen them in my room. They made me fall in love with myself, with my beautiful body. Even now I look at them and they return to me what the sad men take away.

"A man who can make you fall in love with yourself. I was seduced by the pictures, by posing. I love being painted, it's almost as if the badger-hair brush were sliding across my skin rather than the canvas. To be wholly seen, not just as breasts and buttocks. But paintings are after all decorations on the soul of the painter and soon I fell in love with the man himself, with his madcap jabber while he sketched, his uncanny stare, the fury and deftness of his lovemaking."

But how had this fresh-faced, fleet-footed, flame-haired girl come to toil in a tiny room beneath a succession of despondent men?

Artists are slaves to attention and lacking an audience their gestures are the knocking of dead twigs in a barren brake. So one night as she frolicked above the boulevard, a sword-swallower whose audience had dropped off so sharply the only thing that had entered his stomach for three days had been cold steel, stepped onto the shoulders of his friend the strongman and swiped Solya's rope in two.

She would have died had she not landed flukily in a barrow of chrysanthemums but even so she broke both legs.

Zarko tended her while she recovered, brewing soup and telling jokes. Her bones were a long time knitting and when finally she could put weight on them she discovered they'd healed unevenly. One leg was shorter than the other and she'd always walk with a limp. But most awful, her livelihood was stolen from her for she'd lost her equilibrium and could no longer walk the rope.

"To lose what you love," she lamented. "I had nowhere to turn. For days I wandered lonely through the streets even as you had when you first arrived."

"But Zarko?"

"I could no longer walk the rope, don't you see? Zarko had fallen in love with an image of bright hair against the stars. That girl was gone. He no longer loved me, he no longer painted me."

"He forsook you because of your injury? Has he no honor?"

She regarded him curiously. "If one falls in love with a butterfly and it enters a cocoon and emerges a caterpillar has one an obligation to continue loving that creature?"

"But surely your high-wire dancing was not all he loved. What about your pretty face, your hair? What about your voice?"

"Thank you, Pico. But no, a loved one may not be chipped into fragments like a statue. Certainly my face and voice have altered now that I am no longer an acrobat."

"But your hair hasn't changed color."

She smiled. "He still allows me to go to him, you know. He'll even fuck me if he's drunk enough. He's my whore, I pay by finding him pretty girls to paint."

"How can you stand it?"

"At least I'm near him, at least he'll touch me, even if the touch is a slap. And there is this. He forbids me to take another lover."

Pico looked at her bewildered. "But you take other lovers nightly."

"They are my work. They're no threat to him. But if I should sleep with a man for any reason other than money he would be furious."

"I don't understand."

"Neither do I. But I take some comfort in the fact that I can still arouse emotion within him."

They were silent awhile, Solya looking at the smashed glass on the cobbles where Zarko had thrown his bottle.

"But how did you end up in the whorehouse, Solya?"

"This town is not sympathetic to failed tightrope walkers or young girls without family. If we don't starve we find our way eventually to that secret house. But sometimes, sometimes I dream I'm above the boulevard, fires in my fists, sustained only by the applause below, my dancing feet riding the adoration of the multitudes."

Later that day he walked with Solya between the tilted houses tucked among the rocks, up where they could gaze across the city and fields and forest and see the sun sucked into the distant trees. Some minutes they stood watching the sunset and he said, "Beyond the last trees a winged girl I once kissed rides the wind above the sea."

Then Solya led him to a house more crooked than the others, propped like a warped book between two sturdier buildings. Its walls caved and bulged disconcertingly, the door she knocked upon a misdrawn trapezoid, its edges so often shaved to accommodate shifting post and lintel.

Zarko opened the door rubbing his eyes and ushered them into the delicious fumes of linseed oil, turpentine, varnish. "Welcome to chaos," he shouted. Among the detritus of crumpled and trodden paper were hillocks of wrung tubes and clotted brushes, jars of tinted liquids.

The walls were clad in a lichen of old paint, the few sections of bare plaster intricate with drawings. Canvases leaned facing the walls, charcoal sketches were tacked about along with a number of paintings, mostly of young girls. All softnesses and a common quality of pensiveness as if the sitter were spied on alone in a room at the end of a dolorous day. It seemed incredible that work of such clarity could emerge from such havoc. But Pico knew that poems often surfaced from similar middens of mental discards, the throwaway thoughts and slips of the tongue that accumulated in the gutters of the brain and pieced themselves miraculously into a new and strange coherence. He turned to Zarko searching for a way to express the tenderness the images aroused but the artist was already impatiently motioning him to a stool in the center of the room.

"May I stay, Zarko?" Solya asked but he shook his head without looking at her. She smiled sadly at Pico, then slipped quietly out.

Pico sat with a book in his lap but not reading, surrounded by the giddy walls, while the painter littered the floor with charcoal sketches. Zarko crushed the charcoal sticks into the paper and was forever rummaging for more in a box beside him, his hands and face black where he'd dashed sweat away. A sooty halo about his head. "Hold still," he shouted constantly though Pico imagined he sat stonelike. At last he began working more slowly over one drawing, manipulating the charcoal with finger and fist, skimming the stick over the surface. He ripped the sketch from the easel and tacked it to the wall. "There!" he exclaimed. "There's something we can work with." He'd caught the lines of Pico's face with scant strokes so judiciously placed there could be no mistaking the features for another's. The eyes blank, lending a faraway expression. Shading only on the coat and hat.

"Sitting's hard labor, my models tell me," Zarko said, plunging head and hands into a basin of water. He toweled dry on a scrap of canvas. "Let's go get something to eat."

As they walked to the boulevard Pico asked what he did with the paintings he completed.

"I give them away, or keep them if I'm fond of them. Sold art corrupts. Solya said you're a poet. Could you sell a poem?"

"Never," said Pico. "It would be like selling a child."

"Precisely."

"But then how do you survive?"

"Ah. You'll see. There's only one means of making money appropriate to an artist. Come along."

They reached the boulevard at the height of the evening promenade, the crowds noding and swirling about the braziers and performers. Zarko seemed enthralled by the entertainers, wriggling into the throngs around a snake charmer, a magician dragging doves from his hat, identical twins singing canons, a woman whose ferret leaped through tiny hoops of fire. He yelled and gesticulated, turning to his neighbors and clapping their backs, guffawing, while Pico looked on amused by his companion's capers.

After a few minutes of antics Zarko flung an arm around Pico's shoulder and led him away down the center of the avenue. He pulled a fat pouch from his cloak and dropped it clanking into Pico's palm. "How's that for an evening's work?" he grinned. Pico gaped. "But how?"

"Look at me." Zarko turned Pico to face him.

"Yes?" Pico asked.

"Notice anything different?"

"No. Well. Were you wearing a hat earlier?"

"Look at the hat, fool."

Pico snatched a hand to his bare head. "It's——. You——. How did you do that?"

"What about this book. Recognize it?"

Pico took back the volume of poems he'd been carrying in his coat.

"You're a pickpocket!"

"Sh. Don't tell the whole street. Let's see if this loot can get us some supper."

They ordered a massive meal at an outdoor restaurant. Peppercorn pate on toast to begin, then bowls of mushroom soup. Sautéed steaks in a cream and brandy sauce, buttered noodles, green beans with garlic, and for dessert Zarko ate strawberry ice cream made using snow gathered on the mountainside and Pico ordered a wedge of yellow cake soaked in rum, scattered with raspberries. They each drank a bottle of wine, and when they leaned back groaning Zarko snapped his fingers at the waiter and demanded a decanter of their finest cognac. Then he pulled from his pocket a flat tin of cheroots and offered one to Pico.

"That was amazing," Pico said. "The best meal I've had in months."

"Ah yes," Zarko said, belching profoundly, seizing the iron candlestick to light the cigars. "This is the life for an artist."

"Do you steal only from the rich?" Pico asked.

"I steal from anyone idiot enough to leave their coins where I can reach them. They owe it to me. I make their lives more beautiful. My paintings have changed the way this city sees, their very faces have been altered by my eyes."

"I'm sure mine has been," Pico said politely.

"Daily my eyes steal beauty and return it enhanced."

"I was a thief once. But not a very good one." He told Zarko about his adventures with the robber band.

"All artists are thieves. All art is thievery. But pickpocketing is the pinnacle of robbery. Sneaking through houses at night in a cacophony of snoring, where's the skill in that? But stealing from a person's very garments while he's standing next to you, now that's an art. Of course a painter would make a better pickpocket than a poet. My fingers are more accustomed to deceit. I don't lie with my tongue but I lie on paper and canvas and the world succumbs to my untruths so that they become truths."

"Poems are lies as well."

"I believe them so they must be."

"Are you in love with the girls you paint?"

"Of course. And the boys. Why else would I paint them?"

"You're in love with me?"

"Your eyes are not from this city. They are mythic eyes, eyes of the forest, eyes of the sky. They hold images this city has never even dreamed of. I am in love with strangeness."

"You were in love with Solya once."

"Ah Solya, Solya. If you'd seen her afloat on a river of light above the boulevard, a girl on fire. . . . No one was not in love with her. I approached her the only way I knew how, as a pickpocket. After her performance one night, as she moved through the crowd eating strawberries from a paper cone, I followed her and sidled my hand into her gold trousers. But as soon as my fingers had entered the cloth I realized my mistake for my knuckles encountered not flimsy fabric but bare flesh. The pocket was no cotton pouch but a portal to a woman's body. And what a body. I'm not one to linger if I err but even through my blind fingers I could tell the skin was the color of starlight, of winter breath. I moved my hand from her flank to her buttocks and farther down where I could feel fire and she did not pull away but wriggled deeper into my probe. My eyes unseeing for once, all sight in my fingertips until at last I turned and looked into her face, her giggle.

"'I'm a pickpocket,' I blurted, and she said, 'Well, now you've snitched my snatch, what are you going to do?'

"I took her back to my studio but we didn't make love that night, though she was naked. She twirled on a rope halfway to the ceiling and I drew and drew, pulling her face toward me. And then I began to paint. The riot of her hair. Ah, nothing else like it in all the world save maybe the sun."

"But you no longer find her beautiful."

"My loyalty is to my heart. My heart follows my eyes and my eyes have moved on."

Over time Pico became familiar with the whores of the house, the tall one with haunches like pumpkins, the pretty midget, the one with three breasts, the one tattooed with flowers like a garden in girl form, the one muscled like a mason, the legless one, the one who wore a muzzle that she not rip out the throats of the men she attended to, the children whose breasts had only just begun to nibble at their blouses, the obese whores and the wraiths, those who swung quirts and hooks, those who brandished feather dusters or soft cords or brass-knobbed walking sticks, purveyors of pain, terror, tenderness.

He was their pet poet, caged above their contortions, and they grinned and winked at him in the hallways and brought him tidbits, buttery biscuits or marzipan pastries they'd baked. And he returned their generosity with careful courtesy though Solya remained the only one he'd go out with.

Narya alone did not smile at him, did not enter his room, though he often saw her watching him from corners, from windowsills as night fell, the slow rise and fall of the ember at the end of her cigarette flagging her form.

He'd been in the whorehouse for two weeks when he approached Solya one evening. "Books," he told her, "I must have books," and she took him to the booksellers who were her friends and Pico squandered his wages on several volumes which he devoured in a couple days and came to her clamoring for a loan to buy more. She laughed to see his hunger and got up from the chair where she'd been mending one of her gaudy costumes. "Come with me," she said.

He followed her through the lounge, deserted at this early hour, where the traces of the night's labors remained, lipstick on the rims of glasses, overflowing ashtrays. She led him into the small triangular cubbyhole behind the staircase and there she lit a candle, stooped and lifted a trapdoor, revealing a black and reeking grotto. In dank darkness they descended, the flame glimmering on slimy stone. Rats on sordid errands paused and peered furtively over their shoulders, roaches skittered across the walls like antic blood clots.

A few paces down the tunnel she stopped before another door on which was blazoned in red: ENTER AT YOUR PERIL. Smoke seeped around the hinges and Pico, imagining dragons, asked, "Is it safe?"

"For us it is," Solya said. She knocked and after a few moments the door cracked open and a lit cigarette poked out.

Beneath the whorehouse, beneath the city, in a disused sewer tunnel, in a cave entirely usurped by books, Narya spent her days a hermit in a cloister of words. Books teetered, a forest of stacked and voiceless language, across the floor. In their midst was a table where candles burned and on the table an enormous pile of paper.

"What do you want?" she glowered.

Solya explained Pico's situation. "Think about it, Narya," she pleaded. "Imagine you've been without books for months and you arrive at a place heaped with books you can't afford."

"I brought three books from my library in the city by the sea," Pico said eagerly. "I'd be delighted to trade."

Narya backed away, sucking on her cigarette, and he was certain she was about to evict them but she leaned against the desk and motioned him to sit on one of the more stable stacks. Her black gaze augured through the smoke. "Books," she said.

"Books," he leaned forward earnestly, hands clasped in his lap.

"Books," she nodded, a ritual word now, and stood and reached a volume down from a shelf.

Solya smiled. "I'll leave you, then," she said.

What it is to encounter one's passion in another. Pico's love of books had seemed so solitary that the chamber of his heart which held that reverence had nearly sealed itself off. The holy library. He'd considered himself aberrant, a freak, like a man who desired creatures of a different species, ewe or doe, rather than human women. But here was a girl on the far side of the world who revered what he did, who lived as he had surrounded by books, words churning always through her mind like water through a mill. Who contained as well the mill-race and the still pool.

Sometimes that night their voices rose to shouts, sometimes they wept. Pico on his belly floundering in pages. Narya struggling under armloads. They dragged from fecund and roiling brains long daggers of sentences, brandishing them like challenges, or flung out single words more precious, more enduring than jewels, scattering them across the floor. Words rolled around like the aftermath of a snapped necklace. Fragments of stories from books and from experience dovetailed so they had no clear idea what manner of outlandish life the other might have lived. And Narya showed him the list of chapter headings of the novel she was writing, which he gathered told the story of a girl who one day packed some sandwiches, tied a flock of starlings to a flower-pot and rose into the sky.

When Solya looked in on them well after midnight she found Narya standing on the table declaiming, "How alien, alas, are the streets of the city of grief," while Pico knelt clutching her ankles. Solya grinned. Narya left off chanting and sucked her cigarette while Pico staggered to his feet wiping his eyes.

"I'm off to the Owl and Anvil," said Solya. "I heard your racket and thought you might want to come."

Narya looked doubtful but Pico seized her hand. "Come, Narya," he urged. "We have to be together this night."

So she got off the desk and blew out the candles and the threesome walked to the tavern under their umbrellas. Zarko was sitting at a corner table and he shouted for them to join him. The chubby proprietor emerged from the murk clutching four steins in each fist, vanished through a doorway and reappeared wiping his hands on his apron, breathlessly demanding their orders.

"Whisky," shouted Zarko but Solya held up her hand. "Let's drink wine tonight. Three bottles of your finest red. Grapes, if you have them. And clean glasses, mind."

"Certainly," and the proprietor dipped back into the foggy clamor.

Pico looked around. Under a square of open sky an immense anvil stood on worn cobblestones and across the walls scythe blades and horseshoes arced, remnants of the tavern's former life. From time to time an inebriate or two mounted the anvil to sing a song, sloshing through the forgotten verses, voices rising with the chorus.

When the wine and grapes arrived and the glasses had been filled, Zarko proposed a toast.

"Blood for the blood of those who worship beauty," he said and they chimed the glasses together and drank and the wine was indeed rich and rusty as blood.

"Worship, not love," said Solya.

"Beauty is my religion," he said, "pretty girls are my idols, I make my own icons." He pulled a sketchbook from his cloak and began to draw.

"What is your religion?" Solya asked Narya and she shook her head, unwilling to answer or perhaps claiming silence as her faith.

"Yours?" to Pico who looked down into his glass. "Wings?" he said. "Books? Sorrow. I am seeking my temple, I suppose, somewhere in the sands of an eastern desert. What about you, Solya?"

She looked around the table. "My friends," she said. "I am in my temple."

"To the holy Owl and Anvil," Zarko intoned and they raised their glasses again.

As the night wore away the bustle and bellow subsided, patrons stumbling out on hazardous expeditions to their beds or simply sprawling along benches or on tabletops or the puddled floor itself. None much older than Pico.

"So many children in this city," he said almost under his breath. "Why are there no old people here?"

"I keep them young," Zarko shouted, overhearing him. "With my paintings I keep them young. As long as I capture the faces of the girls, pin them on paper, they will never die, they'll live forever."

"No one can live forever," said Pico but Zarko was bent over his sketchbook muttering "Forever young, forever young."

"Where do the dead go?" Pico asked.

"We have eaten them," Solya said.

"Don't spew your airy nonsense at me," Zarko cried, flinging a nub of charcoal at her.

"I don't mean metaphorically," she said and turned a grape between finger and thumb. "This was flesh once." She placed it between her teeth and crushed it. "Is flesh again."

Narya stubbed out her cigarette then and stood and mounted the anvil. She raised her hands and recited in her rough voice, slowly as though she lulled a child, her words falling like the onetime sparks off the iron she stood upon.

"Under the city my love lies sleeping,
deep in the dark, deep in the dark,
with coins on his eyes and a stone on his tongue,
sand in his skull and a worm in his heart.
Long ago I ate his eyes, I drank his blood like wine.
His tears have entered every well
and his semen is the sap of peaches.
Under the city my love lies sleeping,
deep in the dark, deep in the dark."

The company shouted and stamped their feet and she glowered at them, stepped off the anvil and slouched back to her chair making another cigarette.

"Let's all perform!" Solya cried and mounted the anvil and sang in her pretty voice a song about a boy who caught a falling star and fell in love with it but when he kissed the star its fiery lips burnt him to a cinder.

"And now," said Zarko, when she stepped down to fervent applause, "our guest must also contribute to the revelry."

"Oh I couldn't," said Pico, "you're all so wonderful," but his neighbors prodded him to his feet and he went to sit on the iron podium, hands clutched between his knees.

"Up," Zarko grinned. "Up, up on the anvil. It's your initiation, you have to follow the rules."

And Pico was made to mount the rusty hulk. Looking to the pane of sky above, where the first stirrings of dawn lived, he sifted through words, closed his eyes, then recited:

"At the end of a small rain,
as shadowed canyons move above me,
a valley shifts, a cliff shears away
and I see a fresh city lifting in the distance,
a city in transient hills.
The last rope falls. I reach out
before it's too late
and pull myself up a raindrop's arc,
my skin stretched like a drumhead
on the cross of my bones,
the wind beating me thinner,
paring me to molecules and desire.
The air's more precious the higher I go.
I sip its receding pleasures.
Among debatable islands I plunge
but these shores have no hold, I will not heed
the cries of the forlorn who stand on the beaches
flinging handkerchiefs into the waves.

I will not stop until I reach the streets of the city

that disintegrates even as I yearn toward it,

the streets of the city at the end of the rain

where you are walking, where you are walking

waiting for my hand."

A second of reverent silence and then they rose, his new friends, with a communal cry like startled seagulls, rose and lifted him from the anvil and bore him on a celebratory circuit of the tavern while he laughed and tried to avoid the rafters and Solya plucked a tulip from the bodice of a prone woman and stuck it in his hat.

When they finally set him back in his chair and Solya had topped the glasses with the last of the wine, Zarko led a solemn toast to the poet who had ported those words from a city on the far side of the world.

Pico thought he'd never been so happy. Clutches of artists had romped through the books he'd read but they'd always seemed fantasy, the wet dreams of lonely writers. Here at last he sat among those who elevated beauty over moneymaking, who revered what he did, holding the subversive jig and squirm of hand and eye and voice in pursuit of loveliness holy above the liturgy of trade and manners that cohered and stifled ordinary lives.

As day broke they waded through the flotsam of slumped bodies, spilled ale, the bitter odor of old cigarettes, and walked in the powdery light to a cafe. Pico ordered a mushroom omelet, fried potatoes, two sausages, a slice of melon and coffee. He'd entered the euphoric country beyond exhaustion where frolic indeed the dreams of eternal life.

"I feel after so long I'm coming home," he informed the group. "Last night was a night out of my wildest longings and now I'm ravenous."

Solya stroked his cheek.

"Those who seek with the heart's eye will always find each other," said Narya. "We bind the world with our words, our travels are our winding-sheets."

"But no one in this city travels," Pico said, puzzled. "Your world is only as wide as the horizon."

"Until you arrived," Solya giggled but Narya looked stern.

"There are those who travel," she said.

"What do you mean?" Pico asked. "Who are the travelers?" But he had lost his audience for the group had turned their heads to the northern end of the boulevard and he realized the street had grown quiet. No clink of coin or scrape of iron chair leg on cobblestone, and now a thin tune trickled to them. The breakfast party rose and he followed them to stand along the boulevard and doors opened and other citizens poured silently out till a deep crowd flanked the street. Solya pulled off Pico's hat, placed it in his hands.

First came flower girls with baskets of lilies and carnations and they gave each watcher a flower and a curtsy. Tears stained their cheeks. Pico clutched a carnation, heart hammering in his ears. It seemed the whole city stood still save this small procession. Next came a young girl wearing a black frock playing a recorder and beside her a small boy in black tails and a bow tie beating a drum. And behind them at the slow pace the children set walked a young man in a white cotton robe and at the sight of his face Pico nearly cried out. It was pale as the snows above with fear, the fear that only the certainty of imminent death can raise. Pico knew the youth stepped toward his doom, whatever it might be, to the tune of a child's recorder and the rattle of a tapped drum.

As he passed, the gathered throngs cast their flowers at the youth. Some struck his robe and fell to the street and others fell before his feet and he trampled them but did not heed the small blows of the blossoms. His eyes were fixed on the sky.

The procession crossed the great bridge and turned up a side street and still they stood listening, the whole city listening in a massive silence to the small faltering notes of the recorder and the thin racket of the drum. The small sad parade moved up among the narrower streets and the leaning houses and after a long time they saw them again among the last houses, the music too distant to hear now. Where the city ended the musicians and flower girls halted and the white-robed youth walked on alone, up the path scrawled through the stones, a scrap of paper, a flake of ash drifting toward the black angles, the dark castle high in the snows.

They left their breakfast half-eaten, unpaid for, and walked back, each alone, to their rooms. But Narya as she passed Pico whispered, "There. You have seen a traveler."

At midnight she came to him and stood in his doorway holding her umbrella and lighting a cigarette. Though she said nothing he closed the book he'd been reading and pulled on his coat and hat and took up his umbrella and they walked out into the rain. The rest of that night they paced together along the banks of the river, leaning on the balustrades of every bridge.

"The bridges are the ribs of this dead city," she said.

"The ribs are a ladder to the city's sad heart," he replied.

"I come here to be lonely." She looked down into the current.

"Bridges are between places, they bend through time and space and who knows on what shore they'll cast you."

"Other shores. I haven't known them."

Pico looked at her. "You will know them."

"Only the last shore."

"Which we all walk toward."

"The people in your city by the sea, do they live forever?"

"No one lives forever, Narya."

She looked at him, shook her head. "Your city's so strong inside me, I see it like a painting, the towers, the bells, the winged people like flecks of gold leaf on the blue. I see girls bent over balconies, and the patrons of restaurants beneath striped awnings, and children in the parks and all are young forever. A pair of lovers is kissing there and will never part lips. The spiced dishes on the tables will remain eternally fragrant and the winged people will never fall from the sky. Forever young, forever young. Zarko said it. Is it not so, Pico? Tell me it's so in your country."

"We die, Narya, we die."

But she had begun to weep and so did not hear him and he held her body to his. He felt it suddenly best that she not relinquish her version of his city for his vision of his own zenith, Paunpuam, had remained intact though some had attempted to dissuade him from it.

Perhaps indeed by her will the city by the sea remained outside time, the same wave beating the same sands forever.

"What will keep us from casting ourselves into the river?" she said.

"Our task. Your task and mine, the quarrying of poems."

"The quarrying of poems. Where shall we erect them, what graves will our poems stand above, stone wings folded? In what mossy cemetery, Pico?"

"Stone wings can also fly, stone arms can hold us. As Solya said, a body lost to us is life for the worms."

At dawn she led him to a small cemetery at the edge of the city, sequestered under old trees where drops fell continually from the gray hanks of moss and mist lingered in corners where the wind could not lick it away. The stones stood nearly concealed, the inscriptions they'd borne now shallow dents under lichen. No birds, the only movement the falling drops and the stately choreography of a spider mending a web. Narya knelt beside one of the stones.

"I've brought you here to tell you a story," she said. "A story about perseverance. The indomitability of love. Nineteen years ago, as a shopkeeper in the city was closing up, tidying the shelves and reckoning the day's accounts, a white-faced woman in a soiled dress came into his store, her hair muddy as though she'd been slogging through a swamp. She said no word but pointed to a bottle of milk on a shelf and when he gave it to her she bowed her head and walked away without paying and though he called after her she did not turn. A bottle of milk was no loss for him but he could not erase her face from his eyes. The next night as well she came and again he gave her the milk, thinking she must be desperately poor for she wore the same mud-stained dress. She came the third night and once more he complied with her silent request but this time locked up his shop and followed her through the streets and saw her enter this cemetery. When he came under the trees she had vanished but he heard the distant cry of a child, which he pursued among the gravestones only to hear it grow fainter. He retraced his tracks and realized the cry came from beneath this stone I touch and the stone appeared undisturbed as it is now. Hurrying back to his store he fetched a spade and returned to dig where he still heard the child cry. When he lifted the rotten wood of a coffin lid there was a fat baby sitting on her mother's decaying ribs, bawling, three empty bottles beside her.

"The man took the child and covered the grave again and he put the child in the house where the abandoned girls of this city find their homes. But the girl had not been abandoned, no, her mother had not left her but loved her enough to return from the grave when her breasts had decayed in order to find milk for her daughter."

She stood and thrust her hair from her face.

"You were that girl," Pico whispered and she nodded.

"This was my first home," she said. "It's a quiet place. I often come here."

As they walked back to the whorehouse he pointed to the black house in the snow. "The travelers," he said. "Where do they go?"

But she shook her head. "None has ever returned to tell."

"Who lives there?"

"Stories. All the whispered stories of this sad city live there. But the prince of darkness has no name."

"Or all names."

"He has no name."

He'd been working in the restaurant for a month when a fat fumble-
fingers scorched a crust two nights running and Goyra broke a platter
over the girl's head and shoved her out the door. She turned to Pico.
"You," she shouted. "Skinny boy. I've seen you eyeing my techniques.
Why don't you leave the dishes to drip-dry and try your hand at a
sauce or two." So suddenly he found himself installed as assistant chef.
He had much to learn but cooking over campfires during his months
in the forest had sharpened his dexterity and now he learned to wield
spatulas and whisks as deftly as he could a pen. And Adevi had taught
him how to handle a knife.

He learned the delicate art of the omelet, of the fragility of fresh
cream and the vagaries of the egg yolk. He learned to tend a copper
pan with its washing of tin. He learned the foundations for sauces, the
combinations of flour, stock, butter, wine, yolk, and all the flavorings
in various combinations.

"I've never married," said Goyra, "though not for lack of offers, a
man's stomach is his most neglected erogenous zone, but I perform
marriages every day." And she taught him how kidneys revel in a mus-
tard sauce, how a simple cream sauce with a few drops of lemon could
enhance the trout that inhabited the mountain brooks, how a fine cognac flamed over steak seared flavor into the meat.

And he learned of wines. She took him to her cellar and showed
him the bottles in their nooks, cobwebbed, some undisturbed for gen-

erations. One evening she chose an ancient bottle, cradled it gently as she might a baby up the stairs, uncorked it and set it to breathe on a side table. That night when the last of the diners had reeled out the door she poured two fat glasses and led him through the sniffing, the swilling, the chewing of the liquid. The wine she served was over a century old and Pico thought the essence of that span was captured in its bouquet for the drinking of the wine was like a distillation of life itself, so many complex emotions contained within it. He talked about himself while she sipped dourly, about his city by the sea and the journey he'd taken to get to this place and the meals he'd eaten along the way. She watched him through a scrim of cigarette smoke and mocked him at first, "Most epicures are mad, I am myself," but when he began to expound on the dishes of the city by the sea she realized no imagination could have contrived the outlandish concoctions he described, the lobsters grilled with artichoke hearts and tarragon, the crabs with fresh ginger, the fish poached in coconut milk, the rice spiced with saffron, cloves and cardamom, speckled with raisins. Then she grew animated and made him relate the ingredients of each dish in as much detail as he could, though he lamented that he'd lived mostly on bread, goat cheese and pickled mushrooms.

That night as they drank, this woman, crushed as the butts she discarded, visage ghastly as a crusted cauldron, confided that she had sold her looks to the devil in exchange for his recipes.

"What's a pretty face when faced with fabulous pastry?" she said. "Oh I was a pleasant sight once, long-legged, breasts firm and sweet as flan, and all the lovely boys salivated at the sight of me. Beauty is like an egg though, delicious when fresh but too soon rancid. So when the devil stepped into my dreams one night as he does sooner or later into the nighttimes of each of us, I begged him to give me something that would last beyond my youth. He bestowed upon me this talent," and she reached to a bowl of fresh wafers and placed one to melt, butter-tender, on Pico's tongue. "But the devil is a salesman and he does not bestow his gifts at random. No, I bought this gift at a price." She passed her fingers across her face as though she'd pull the skin away.

"Your hands are beautiful," Pico said, and she growled and sucked her cigarette so he knew she was pleased.

"Must I sell my looks to learn your art?" he asked, at which she chortled. "No, no, just give me some of your time. And maybe we can fatten you up in the process," and she ran a thumb down the glocken-spiel of his ribs.

So he played apprentice sorcerer to the dwarf chef and she whispered to him recipes learned, she insisted, from a pale man with a pointed beard who, when he doffed his hat, displayed two horns, ridged and rigid as shells among his curls. A merchant, purveyor of earthly pleasures, but at a price, at a price.

And truly her dishes were redolent of sin, succulent with guilt.

With Narya in her lair. He'd brought back several borrowed books and had come to get more and also read some of the novel she was writing. She would not allow the manuscript out of the room but let him sit and read a chapter at a time. It was like plowing through the forest, so tangled the scrawl, detours wandering all around the page so he was constantly twisting and turning the paper, the trail sometimes evading him so he had to retrace his steps and set off again paying closer attention. A taxing slog but infinitely rewarding as the story was the most marvelous he'd ever read.

THE PLANET OF BOOKS

As the traveler descended to the pale planet she heard a whisper, welcome to her ears, a whisper that she could not place. It was not the sound of falling water nor the sound of breathing nor the sound of wind in leaves, though it was close to all of these. But this sound evoked interiors, a fireplace, a mug of cocoa, rain on dark windowpanes. As her starlings gusted downward she saw below her flocks of other birds winging over the treetops, and even from far above she sensed they were unlike the birds she knew, and the trees seemed strange, as if they had too many leaves. But it was not until she was almost among the branches that several of the strange birds flew past with a riffling whir and she realized they were not birds after all, but books, books freed from fingers and shelves, flapping unfettered through the air. She saw that the trees bore, instead of green leaves, the dry, pale leaves of books, like many-petaled flowers fondled by the wind. This was the whisper of course, that was not quite water or breath or leaves, it was the ruffle of ten thousand turning pages. All across the planet pages turned in the wind.

Tugging on the strings that harnessed her starlings to the flowerpot, she guided her terra-cotta craft to a landing in a little clearing and disembarked. Flowers spattered the grassy circle, small squarish blooms, which, when she knelt, she realized were tiny volumes of poetry, exquisitely bound, with gilt-edged pages and marbled endpapers. The grass was printed too with lines of verse, and she browsed among them, lying with her chin propped on her palm, running her fingers through shredded iambic pentameter. Booklets wafted like butterflies flower to flower and when one lit on her wrist and fanned its pages she read a dainty haiku. After a while she set off through the forest, though she made little headway as she was constantly stopping to muse on odes etched into tree trunks or leaf though a half-decayed book dropped from a tree. Some of these fallen volumes were so sweet they made her light-headed, others so sour she felt queasy after she read them.

She came upon a dappling of mushrooms, or books that grew like mushrooms, in a dark corner beneath great trunks, with their spines upward, their leaves hanging toward the soil. She was careful to avert her eyes, not knowing which were poisonous.

Eventually, browsing through this world of words, she came in the afternoon to a meadow where several dozen massive books lay splayed open on the grass, and in the center of their pages, along the creases, lay beings like herself, asleep. As she watched they sat up and stretched and rubbed their eyes and reached for their spectacles. She saw that they wore garments sewn up of printed pages, pleated and ruffled, with sprays of torn paper blossoming from sleeves and cuffs, and folded paper caps, and they rustled when they moved. All wore thick spectacles, which made their eyes enormous. They did not seem surprised to see her, but invited her to join them and tell her story. This she was pleased to do, sitting on the cover of a fat book and relating her journey thus far, and as she spoke they watched her with huge dreamy eyes.

When she was done with her tale and had listened to several sonnets and snippets of ballads, they began to wander off in various directions, muttering about lunchtime. She as well was hungry, and decided to follow one group as they descended to the river, for they bore nets in their hands. But when she crouched on the banks beside them and peered into the water she saw that the creatures which moved there, wavering their pages like fins or gills, were not fish but books, their covers pebbled like the river bottom. Some were tiny and swam in groups, flicking this way and that, but others moved alone, ponderously, and it was these the book folk aimed for with their nets. When a heap of heavy, dripping tomes lay on the bank, some pages still flipping idly over, they put their nets aside and, stretched out on the printed grass, began to read, inviting the traveler to join them. This she did, though her stomach rumbled and she was disappointed they had not scooped up a trout or salmon to grill. But when she lay among the other readers and began turning the sodden pages, she soon sank deep within the story, so deep in fact that several times she had to lift her eyes for fear of drowning. This river book was the strongest, most satisfying book she'd ever read, full of blue light and rapids and deep, dark pools, and when she'd finished, replete, she lay back and slept, submerged in currents and shadows. She realized when she woke that she was no longer famished, that the book had somehow taken the edge off her hunger. And now she knew that on this planet of books hunger was not sated through the mouth but through the eyes, and she thought this a much more satisfactory means of acquiring nourishment.

Over the next days she partook of the winged books she had seen in her descent, which made her dizzy with their soaring prose, and she read the delicately flavored volumes plucked from certain trees, spiced with collections of pungent aphorisms gathered from certain bushes, and she savored prized books of poetry, printed in silver on black vellum, dug from among certain roots. She even learned to tell which of the mushroom books were safe, and was glad she had been wary, for the dreamy readers told dreadful tales of companions who had choked before their eyes, going into spasms as they perused the wrong toadstool.

On this diet of incessant reading and conversations with her companions, who were forever sidestepping into fantasy or flights of poetry, she began to lose her own sense of the real. She became unsure whether she woke or dreamed, whether the hand she held up was her hand or a hand from a book she read, and this sensation, though initially disconcerting, was not unpleasant.

Sometimes late at night the book folk told terrifying tales of strange rare books that roamed the deep forest, and at the heart of these was always the carnivorous book, a huge tome, its leather dappled gold and black. It was seldom seen, and those who did see it seldom lived to tell the tale. When this book opened its great covers a reader would be drawn inexorably within, into the pages printed in red ink that never seemed to dry. The unwitting victim would move closer, mesmerized, desperate, despite dry tongue and quaking knees, to read on. And then, with a snap and a crackle, the carnivorous book would close its pages and the reader would vanish.

Yet there were young people among the book folk not sated by the tame forest diet that sustained their parents, who from time to time left the safety of the clearing and sought out this savage book. For it was said that those few words one managed to read in the moment before one was consumed, that single red page or paragraph or sentence, was worth all the books in the world.

The traveler could have stayed on this planet forever she thought, reading, gathering books, hunting for books, and for a wonderful afternoon she even contemplated seeking the carnivorous book in the depths of the forest. It seemed a glamorous way to die. But her starlings were growing restless and there were other planets to explore. She could see those worlds between the printed leaves at night, as she lay on the soft pages of an open book, glimmering like illegible words in the sky. Also, she was afraid that if she stayed on this world any longer her own story might be lost, submerged into the others until she no longer remembered who she was or where she came from. So, though they beseeched her to stay, she bade farewell to her bespectacled companions and made her way back to the little clearing where her starlings stirred and chirruped, and stepped into her waiting flowerpot. But before she left she plucked a flower, a pretty little volume of poetry to put in her pocket like a fancy chocolate to nibble at, a keepsake from this strange, wonderful planet of living words.

Pico looked up from the pages and rubbed his eyes, returning to the world, to this cellar where a sullen whore wrote such lovely words. He cleared a space among the books and set out a picnic lunch he'd brought, laying a checkered cloth on the floor and placing upon it a wedge of the blue-veined odoriferous cheese he'd become addicted to, a tomato, a cucumber, a loaf of crusty brown bread, butter, peaches, a bottle of white wine. He tapped Narya on the shoulder, startling her from the throes of scribbling, apologized and pointed to the lunch. She stared at the spread, then at him.

"Where did this come from?"

Pico laughed. "When did you last eat?"

She seemed slightly taken aback. "I can't recall. But I've just been describing a banquet in minute detail so perhaps I'm hungry."

Pico uncorked the wine and sliced the bread and cheese and vegetables. Narya nibbled at a slice of cheese then sat back with her wine and lit a cigarette.

"How long have you been writing your book?" Pico asked.

"The story has always been there, I think I was born with it inside me. When I'm at my best it's as though I simply copy the words from some inner manuscript unscrolling behind my eyes. I learned to read very young, in fact I can't remember not knowing how to read."

"Nor can I," Pico smiled.

"I learned to read before I could walk and of course writing follows reading as talking follows hearing. And even those first phrases I crafted painstakingly in crayon on scraps of butcher paper were gestures toward this story."

"It's so different from the poems you recite."

"The poems are weapons. Knives and arrows."

"Yes, I see. When will the novel be finished?"

"When I die, I suppose. I only have one story to write as do we all and I will write it as long as I live. Each chapter is self-encompassing so if I'm taken the book will end with the last chapter I wrote."

"If you're taken." Pico's heart lurched at those words for the fear of the slim seldom-traveled road and the black house had swelled within him. "If you're taken," he repeated. "Where do they go, the chosen ones? Where does the desolate procession send them?"

"All is rumor. It's why we write, it's why we sing, it's why we make love here in this city, enraptured and captivated by fear. For generations we have lived with the knowledge that some must ascend to the dark castle that the rest may have this life of love and song, fine food, stirring literature."

"But don't you want to be free?"

"Why do you think I write?" She tapped the chapter he'd been reading. "I travel far from this city's winding streets in these pages."

"And you never get lonely cooped up with your manuscript?"

"Lonely? Sometimes I can hardly sleep my characters chatter so, clamoring to have their voices immortalized."

Narya came first, late at night, slipping into his bed like a settling cinder, scent of ashes and wine. A soft and potent scorching, smoke from a stick of incense curling across his skin. That first night she said nothing at all, only a single moan escaped her lips. He fell asleep again after she left and in the morning wondered whether she'd even come at all but when he pressed his face to the pillow he whiffed her charred odor.

Then Solya. Sleepy as a kitten she drifted like a stray sunbeam through his door one morning. "I dreamed you were kissing me," she said.

"I'd love to kiss you," he whispered, still in the debatable land where dreams soak into the day, the pale marshes of sunrise. A candle burning at both ends, she stepped from her nightgown and entered the den of his sheets and pressed her lips to his.

"Yes," she said after a while, "that's what I dreamed about."

"Do you make all your dreams come true?"

"If the reality's lying a flight of stairs above me."

"Am I just another of your circus acts, Solya?"

"Yes. I'm a juggler and you are the torch in my hand at this moment. Soon I'll fling you into the sky like a star."

"You're the torch," he plunged his hands into her hair.

"Don't burn yourself," she said.

There was no haste with her, his hands lingering, her lips lingering, as though parts of their bodies were still asleep. Sunlight fell on the bed from the window that opened onto the balcony. By the time they dressed and went to a cafe for breakfast it was afternoon.

"Solya," Pico said over waffles and coffee.

"Yes?"

"Zarko is my friend. What will I tell him?"

"Nothing."

"What if he asks?"

"Lie. Zarko is mad."

"But."

"Pico."

"Yes?"

"Hush."

He had so many friends now in the whorehouse his reading was forever interrupted by girls bearing little cakes or crustless sandwiches but really wanting to talk. And he loved to hear them, loved the intrigues of the whores, their tinsel and rosewater existences, lives of incessant tears and lies, the occasional pretty minute a minuscule reward for the horrors of vending their bodies. They came because he didn't require lipstick to desire their stories. By his side on his mattress they sat and he poured them coffee and they nibbled the dainties the girl had brought, she usually eating more than he, she doing all the talking. And when the plate was empty she'd tip the crumbs over the balustrade, kiss his cheek and descend to her room to prepare to meet the other men, the men who'd pay to tell their stories.

In the forest he'd craved company but here he needed time alone, so many mornings he'd take a book and his notebook and fountain pen and buy apples and bread and blue cheese. And if the day was fine he'd walk up above the city to the littered rocks where the river came tumbling and sit on a warm stone and read.

Though he carried his notebook everywhere, the first two months in that city he could write nothing at all, so new were the words he read. The books he'd been reading all his life felt like the same stories subtly metamorphosing so he'd begun to feel there was only one story, a story that rose common and strange from every vein. But now he felt he'd been living in a room he thought was sealed and he woke one day and realized there was a door in the wall and behind the door a marvelous garden sprawled replete with queer flowers and unknown beasts.

He read the books Narya lent him and some smoldered like lit pine knots in his brain and these he bought with his restaurant earnings if he could find copies in the booksellers' wardrobes for he felt nothing equaled rereading a loved book. Slowly his shelves filled.

On rainy days he went to a cafe and ordered coffee and pastries and read and watched the rain on the window and the blurred shapes of the passersby cowering under their umbrellas. The cafe was warm and steamy and fragrant with coffee and chocolate and cinnamon and full of others sheltering from the rain with their books, looking up often at the drowned glass.

One day Solya found him there and she sat and ordered cocoa and asked what he thought of with such sad eyes.

"The sound of the rain on the roof reminds me of the sound of the sea. This is a cozy sound though, sitting warm in a cafe drinking coffee. Sitting by the sea is ever so lonely, looking out to the horizon where the sky lies like the upper lip of a mouth keeping a secret."

"What's beyond the horizon?"

"Islands. I've read about them. Ships arrive from the islands having weathered enormous storms, having encountered sea beasts big as houses, and they off-load cargos of tea and dyed cloth, blown glass and birdcages, gold and exotic perfumes. They leave nearly swamped under loads of teak and ebony, cotton, pearls, nutmegs, silks. The sailors in their salt-stained britches and eye patches, weapons strung across their torsos, swagger through the city seducing the maidens, relating outlandish tales, singing chanteys, firing pistols into the sky. I'd sit sometimes at the docks where the water gobbled at the pilings and listen to their shouts, their crass and spicy speech.

"Some islands out there, the most distant, still harbor readers and authors. The merchants knew there was a small market for books in the city by the sea, for though the people did not read, the authorities, following ancient precedent, still supported the library with funds to purchase books. And so, reading their wares, I got to know those island towns as well as I knew my own, the low thatched houses and bays crowded with the painted boats of fishermen, the windy hills behind the towns where goats cry, where grapevines weave and olive trees stretch rheumatic arms. These are the islands of the poets. The poet who lives in a square tower above a sea-bashed outcropping, the poet who inhabits a dovecot, his manuscripts nearly illegible under bird droppings, the fisherman poet and the sailor poet, the poet who declared himself king of his island, the blind poet whose every word is scribed by a legion of fanatic followers. Some may still be alive. I alone knew of them, for my library was unused save as a shelter for cats to raise their kittens. Only Sisi, my Sisi, learned to read, learned to love the flow and whimsy of written words."

Solya leaned her elbows on the table, fists under her chin. "Tell me about Sisi."

"She has wings and I do not. Have you known jealousy? That ache which seems so sweet, but pries with its little blades. The kiss is the keenest dagger."

"Do you wish you hadn't kissed her?"

"Would my life have been easier? I'd have pottered around my library perfectly contented till I died. But my heart would never have started beating. I can't wish myself unborn. Now I am in the world and there are no steps backward, as I have learned on this journey."

Solya nodded. "The first step onto the tightrope must carry you to the other side. There is no turning back."

The rain was falling harder and more people had entered the cafe, their umbrellas canting in puddles by the doorway.

Pico leaned forward so she could hear him over the hum from the other tables. "You are walking a tightrope. Between Zarko and me."

She sighed. "I can't live my life without balance and danger, it seems. If there was no stealth, no dainty tiptoe work, I'd be walking a solid floor and that's no challenge."

"In the city by the sea I would not have been able to imagine desiring someone other than Sisi, but on this journey I have learned the heart has many rooms."

"What is love anyway?"

"Love is drinking coffee in a warm cafe on a rainy day and remembering wings above the sea."

"Love is a rope stretched between hearts. I walk from one to the other but where I'm happiest is in between."

"A sword-swallower once slashed that rope."

"But this one's invisible."

"The hearts it adheres to are not."

"Hush. You'll jinx the magic. You're privy to the performance, don't try to see through the illusion that keeps me aloft."

"I'm sorry." But he looked into the dregs of his coffee with foreboding as though the weather that scrabbled at the window had suddenly stepped into his heart.

With Narya long after midnight, long before dawn. The hour when only cats and lovers stir. She was in his arms and he realized she was weeping. He touched the tears away with his tongue.

"Why are you crying?"

She burrowed her head into his embrace.

"Narya, why?"

She pulled away and sat up, hands to her cheeks. Diamonds on her fingertips. "Pico," she said in her corroded voice, "Pico, do you ever feel there is some other way, long ago or somewhere else? Why do certain pieces of music move us so, all of us? Certain colors? As if these were stones from an earlier city, passed hand to hand across the generations so now they're polished and rounded as river stones and yet have lost none of their weight. I feel we're all trying to find a story, like treasure buried beneath our city, and all the feeble stories we live are patterned after that pristine story whose shape we almost know. Sometimes just after I wake or before I make love I'll think, This is the story, I'm living the story. But the world always rushes in with its clash and anguish. Can you hear me, Pico? These are dangerous words for me, they make me feel more naked than when I spread my legs for a stranger."

"The poems I love evoke in me the nostalgia for that story, the buried story."

"And you are walking toward a mythic town to keep that story intact."

"I'm walking to the morning town of Paunpuam to get my wings."

"Why don't you print your poems?" Solya asked after he'd read to her one night. "One of my clients owns a press, he could make a chapbook. They would sell, your voice is so new, so strange."

"If you want me to write out a poem for you, Solya, I will."

"But you could make money, you could buy more books for your shelves."

"I have enough to eat and Narya's library contains a lifetime's supply of literature. Narya herself contains a lifetime's supply of literature. I don't write my poems for gold."

"Why do you write them?"

"Why do women have children? To see my soul spread its wings, to hear my voice from beyond the boundaries of my skin."

"But couldn't you sell them as well?"

"Tell me, what am I to you, Solya? You don't ask me to pay for our nights of love."

"Of course not."

"Why?"

"It would change the nature of our lovemaking."

"But not for me. I'd gladly give you money, stories, jewelry, whatever you desired, just to keep your pretty face next to mine in the long nights, to taste your kiss."

"For me it would change. I wouldn't know if I came to you because I craved your body or a new ribbon for my hair."

"Yes."

"So your poems are love affairs."

"With all the squabbles and separations love affairs entail. And all the kisses."

"Kisses mean nothing." She glanced at him sidelong, sly.

"You are right. They mean nothing."

"Do you know what I mean, really, Pico?" She propped herself on an elbow and looked at him.

"I think I do. The same word may by used in two poems. But in one poem it is sad and lovely and in the other flimsy. What matters are the motions of the heart beneath the hand that holds the pen. My pulse may somehow enter my pen, the ink itself is my blood, the pen an open vein on the page."

"You do understand. A kiss is not a kiss."

"Is not a kiss is not a kiss."

So he learned to know them as lovers, learned to know that portion of themselves by which they made their living. The creatures we are unclothed, in bed, are so often foreign to what we are in the day. Our eyes change color, our gestures alter, our very language shifts and stirs. He learned the delicate vocabularies of their moans, rubies strung along the thread of the night. Their tongues were fingers fettered to their minds, they sang slow silent duets.

Sometimes it seemed they changed above him, beneath him. "Who are you?" he whispered. After lovemaking he read poetry aloud in an effort to fill the silence. They clamored for tidings of the wider world so he told them stories from the forest, from the books of his library.

"Why do you come to me?" he asked. "I do not pay. Why do you bring your gifts to me?"

Solya kissed him and said, "You are a stranger," but Narya only smiled and touched the iris on his upper arm. If his eyes were closed they wore different faces.

He woke one morning and thought his eyes had opened too far. An odd brightness to the walls and he sat up and looked out the window and saw bleached linen draped across every rooftop, brilliant.

He walked onto the balcony into air brisk as a smack, the cold like peppermint in his nostrils, and he went back in and put on his coat and went out again. The alley beneath him a white carpet perforated by the drunken embroidery of a cat's footprints. He scooped a scant handful of snow from the ribbon on the balustrade and tasted it. Flavor of frozen stars. Bringing the brazier onto the balcony he tipped the old ashes into the air and lit fresh charcoal from a hoarded ember.

Solya burst onto the balcony as he was pouring the coffee. She swiped the cigarette from his lips and sucked in smoke as though she were inhaling the light. She was barefoot, wore only her nightgown.

"It's so pretty," she cried, sitting on his lap. "Remember the first day you woke up in my room and I was singing a song?"

"Sing it again."

"Overnight the snow has fallen." Her voice like a scatter of sugar in the frozen air. *"A white shroud I welcome."*

He made another cigarette and they took turns sipping from the coffee mug. She snuggled against his chest and curled her feet under her thighs and he brought the coat about her body but she soon began to shiver so he carried her inside to the sheets, her body a snowdrift upon them.

He imagined the snowflakes were frozen words, falling, telling the secrets the city kept. As the snow settled on the city it seemed to settle as well on his heart and his intentions, numbing them. He'd begun to write again, pallid poems, as though the incessant precipitation of that city in the mountains had watered down the ink so it would not hold to the page.

Often he wished for the loneliness of the forest, the loneliness that allowed him to place valuable words on paper. He had sold his poems for comfort and he was afraid to enter again the trials of solitude. So he wrote poems that lacked heart, written from outside his skin, written in snatches between ale swilling and lovemaking, and he did not allow them to steep, to cure, but read them at once to his friends for the applause they engendered.

Oh that city in the mountains had its temptations. No single aspect of it, no single person within it, would have been enough to hold him there. But together the cafes in the rain and the booksellers' wardrobes and the hundred bridges and the melodies of the street musicians and the ebullience of the taverns and the occasional sapphire skies and Zarko, Solya and Narya, worked a seduction upon him that made him loath to leave. Neither of the whores singly could have offered pleasures enough to hold him but as a pair they satisfied so great a portion of his desires that he almost forgot he lacked love. With Narya he conversed about words and their uses, Solya sang to him, Zarko painted pictures that made him into a prince of poets. Sisi had become an emblem, their story repeated till it had lost its savor. He had sold that story for the respect it afforded him.

And Narya knew. As his poems grew thinner she shied away. He did not pursue her, fearing admonishment, fearing his own guilt.

His quest for the morning town was now a mantra recited to cultivate his otherness. He had abandoned his journey. The thought of leaving his bookshelves and the view of the peaks from his balcony and the coffee and cigarettes in the morning, the nightly ministrations of expert lovers, of quitting these comforts to tramp a forsaken trail to probable death in pursuit of what seemed more and more a whim was repugnant. He shoved the thought from him when it surfaced and each time it stayed under longer.

Who knows how long he might have stayed in that city, cozy, dousing his guilt with wine, cauterizing it with tobacco, had the city remained static. But keep characters in propinquity long enough and a story will always develop a plot.

A flooded field below the city had frozen and bearing brooms and tin trays the four friends walked down and swept the snow from the ice.

It boomed and crackled beneath their tread, and when they had cleared a black expanse like a vast palette of polished obsidian, they carried their trays to the top of the slope. Zarko went first, sitting on his tray, grasping the leading edge like a prow. They shoved him off and, slowly at first, then with a hiss, snow spitting to either side, he sped down. He spun as he hit the ice and scooted across it backward till he plowed into a drift at the far side and lay there kicking and hooting. Solya followed, then Narya, and Pico went last, eyes clenched shut at the speed of his plummet but arriving in Zarko's arms breathless and warm from the thrill. Up the hill they dashed again and flung themselves with more abandon upon their makeshift sleds, plunging at greater velocity as the snow had been tamped to a slick groove. Then again, on their bellies, or back to front, daring each other into more outlandish positions. They went down in pairs, back-to-back, side by side, and Zarko attempted, disastrously, to descend standing upright. As a finale they made a chain of four, clutching each other down the slope but scattering on the ice like seeds from a dropped pod, barreling into the snowbanks, weak from laughter.

Solya had brought a flask of hot chocolate and four mugs and they sat on the trays as she poured the mugs full, the snow retreating in rings about the warm pottery. Zarko pulled a flat bottle from his cloak and added a dollop of rum to each cup and they sat sipping, the heat unfurling through their bones while their cheeks and hands remained against the kiss of frost.

Pico noticed the glow in Solya, not merely the flush from the exertion and excitement but a lapidary sparkle in her eyes that only Zarko could kindle. She taught them rounds and they sang, white breath mingling with the steam from the drinks, Solya's pretty voice and Pico's thin one, Narya's husky rattle and Zarko's tone-deaf howl somehow cohering as if the cold had the property of emulsifying disparate sounds.

They left the trays in the snow and walked back through the city bearing the brooms like itinerant witches, Pico and Narya following behind Solya and Zarko. The city was silent and white, a few windows glowing, and Pico felt like a window himself, warm and radiant, spilling light onto the snow.

Near the top of the city where their ways diverged Solya asked Zarko, in a voice barely above a whisper, whether he needed a companion, whether she should come to his house, but he stopped and turned.

"You will come with me tonight, Narya," he said. "I was watching you, the snow suits your coloring. I will paint you."

Narya shook her head.

"Tell her, Solya," Zarko said without taking his eyes off Narya and Solya went to her and took her hand and turned it and stroked the palm. "For me, Narya," she said, "please. Go with him. I'll pay."

Narya shuddered. She shook free of Solya's grasp and swiveled and walked away.

Solya was suddenly on her knees before Zarko. "What do you want of me?" she wailed. "Tell me what to do, tell me what to do."

"Get away," he snarled and she fell back limp as though he'd kicked her.

That night Pico supported her as she had him how many months before, one upright figure and one wounded walking through a silent city. At the whorehouse he carried her up the stairs and took off her clothes and laid her on a stained mattress. "Sleep," he whispered. "Sleep now, pretty one."

He was woken before dawn by a noise like a coming storm through trees, a banshee shivering through the house below him, wails swirling through every room, spilling out the windows, and he hurriedly put on his dressing gown and went to investigate. Girls cowered in doorways weeping and their clients hauled on trousers and scurried through the hallways.

"What is it, what is it?" Pico asked but the girls ignored him. He went to Solya's room but it was empty and then descended to Narya's chamber but it was locked. He could not discover the cause of the commotion but it had quieted now so he returned to his room, lit a candle and read, though his mind, still aroused by the wailing, refused to focus. At first light he brewed a cup of coffee. What had happened to disturb the girls so? He guessed it was to do with an unruly client, a man who refused to pay or who tried to pummel love from a girl with his fists.

The clamor within the whorehouse having died away, the girls would settle down to their morning naps and in a little while he'd get dressed and go to a cafe for another cup of coffee and a pastry, but now as the peaks flushed and a stealthy sun licked the last smears of night from the sky it was lovely to sit alone and sip coffee. Here and there across the rooftops fraying ropes of smoke lifted but otherwise the city lay still.

Then, sharp as a pebble cracking the brittle air, came a knock in the alley below. He leaned over the balcony to see what naive soul had arrived at the whorehouse at this early hour and not known enough to ring the bell.

Below, foreshortened but still potent enough an image to make his heart stagger, he saw a small boy in bow tie and tails, snare drum strapped at his side, and a young girl in a black frock clutching a recorder. Beyond them at the alley entrance waited the flower girls with their baskets of lilies and carnations.

The girl knocked again and stood back and after a while the door opened and another girl walked out, clad in a white shift belled out at the bosom, her hair a sudden blaze in the snow.

"No," Pico cried. "Solya, I'm coming." And he dashed into his room and down the stairs. But even as he left the balcony he heard the drum and recorder begin to play.

Narya stepped in front of him as he hurtled onto the second landing and he fell with her beneath him and tried to rise again but she twisted her legs about his and her arms about his waist.

"But it's Solya," he wailed.

"Yes," she said, so quietly that he quit his struggle and lay panting and looking at her.

"This morning it's Solya," she said, "and another morning it will be me and another morning it will be you if you stay."

"Is there nothing we can do?"

"Nothing."

He remained for a while, sprawled on the landing, side throbbing, and even through the walls and doors and carpeted hallways of that house he could hear the music of the drum and flute moving higher through a silent city.

Then they mounted the stairs to his balcony and leaned on the balustrade watching the ember of her hair drift slowly away from the houses and rise along the path to the dark mansion and as she neared the walls, a mere spark now, he turned to Narya. His voice shook.

"How are they chosen, those who ascend to the black house?"

"Some are chosen, some choose. Those who wish to leave the city make their desires known to the authorities and the child musicians will arrive to accompany them."

"Solya?"

"Solya chose."

Pico sank to his knees and laid his head on the cold iron and wept. When he looked up Narya was gone and the brindled expanse between the city and the castle was barren of color.

No one would accept his tears, the tears that would not cease, sometimes he woke from dreams to find his face wet. Even Narya turned him away but he beat on her door so long one day that she opened it and stood with a hand on the doorframe.

"Solya," he said and saw the pain skew her brow. She bowed her head a moment and when she looked up her eyes were wet.

"We do not say the names of the dead," she told him.

"But how can we hold them?"

"We might meet them in our dreams."

"Is that enough?"

She shrugged.

"It's not for me. For me it's not enough."

But she shut the door and locked it and no amount of hammering with his fists would make her open it again.

Zarko had entered a fey mood, howling as he hurled paint at canvases, clawing at the colors, rubbing against the paintings so fragments of faces adorned his chest and arms. Pico went twice to his studio and found him gaunt, drunk, eyes puddles of blood. He opened the door to the poet but seemed not to recognize him and went immediately back to his work. The first time Pico sat for a while then left without saying anything. The second time he began to talk but as soon as he mentioned Solya's name the painter plunged his entire torso through the canvas he'd been working on and began to throw himself against the walls, knocking himself comatose before Pico could stop him.

So he took the jar of accumulated coins on his bookshelf and walked to Goyra's restaurant and tipped them out on a table in front of her.

"I want to pay for a meal for three at your restaurant. Your finest recipes. Will these coins be enough?"

She scratched an armpit and bared her lips over teeth the color of fossil bones, then cupped the coins back into the jar and pushed it at him. "Your money wouldn't pay for a bowl of soup," she said and he put his face in his hands.

"I'll work for free, as long as it takes."

"Shut up," she said. "You can have the restaurant any night you wish. I'll cook your friends food that'll make them want to give up sex."

"Goyra, you're marvelous." And he leaned and kissed her tobacco-stained cheek.

The feast began at twilight. Snow was falling. Each of the guests had received an invitation the night before, in gold ink on blue paper, which read: *You are cordially invited to attend a banquet at Goyra's distinguished restaurant, tomorrow at dusk.*

Pico arrived first, followed almost immediately by Narya and Zarko so all three stood in the tiny vestibule a minute stamping the snow from their boots, shaking the flakes from their hats. Pico took their coats and ushered them into the restaurant, which he was surprised to find deserted. An applewood fire snapped in the hearth at one end of the room and a little way back from it, but close enough to receive its heat, a table set for three glowed under a candelabra. Goyra had reserved the restaurant solely for his party this night.

They took seats. At each place silver service, white porcelain, the plates circled with a single blue line at their rims. Two tulip-shaped wineglasses, a fatter glass for brandy. The menu, also gold on blue, was propped against a spray of hothouse violets in the center of the table.

BRAISED ASPARAGUS TIPS WITH A LEMON BUTTER SAUCE

ONION SOUP

ROAST DUCKLING STUFFED WITH SAUSAGE AND CHESTNUTS

GREEN PEAS, PUREED POTATOES, APPLESAUCE

ALMOND CREAM WITH FRESH STRAWBERRIES

At first the friends were shy with one another and they fixed their attention on the food. And what food it was. The asparagus was arranged in green fans on individual plates, the sauce served separately in small bowls. Goyra filled their glasses with a slightly sweet wine that she had chilled on a back windowsill most of the afternoon. They dipped the green arrows into the sauce and avoided each other's eyes, watching instead the fire or the drifting snowflakes in the blue windowpanes.

Then onion soup, dark and fragrant, rounds of toasted cheese bread foundering in the bowls. The only sounds the clink of spoons and smack of lips and small exhalations of delight.

As Goyra collected the soup plates Pico stood to pour more wine then set the bottle on the table and cleared his throat.

"I have lived among you now for half a year in this city in the mountains, city of rain and snow, city of readers and coffee shops. I came here a stranger and you received my poems and my kisses, heard my fears and desires. We are all strangers to each other, but I have come from farther away and the tasks of knowing each of you have been more challenging and thus perhaps more satisfying. What we labor over we cherish. I've learned so much from you, about the art of words, the art of loving. About painting and posing and pickpocketing. I've learned the power of secrets.

"You may believe me naive, but I have learned more than you might think. I know of the taboo against mentioning the names of the dead, of the black house, but here, tonight, I choose to exercise my otherness. Bear with me, I beseech you, this night, for I have called you to this banquet in honor of one who was of our group and has departed. We now lack a voice, a limb of our collective body, we are impoverished because of her absence. I will say her name. Solya. Solya took the seldom-traveled trail to the black house in the snows and she will not return. But we have her memory. We can remember her laugh and her stories and how she loved to eat. Our tendency is always to laud the cerebral but I find with her departure that she taught me much about what it means to dwell in this body, to own this mouth and belly. We need not say her name again but at least let us eat this meal in her memory."

Pico was crying and he sat down abruptly and took a sip of his wine. The other faces at the table had undergone various emotions as he spoke. Fear, shame, anger, relief. Now they sat quietly. Narya cried as well, softly, into her napkin. Their silence was broken by Goyra who banged through the swinging doors bearing an enormous sizzling platter on which lay the roast duckling, the color of varnished mahogany, garnished with apple wedges and sprigs of parsley. Her banter as she carved the bird had just the edge to cut through the shock Pico's speech had induced. She served the guests from bowls of peas and creamy potatoes and cinnamon-sprinkled applesauce. From the shelf where it had stood breathing the last four hours she carried a bottle of red wine and gingerly so as not to disturb the sediment poured each glass half full. Then she retreated to the kitchen where they could hear her rattling dishes and humming tunelessly.

Now came exclamations over the succulent duck with its herbed stuffing and it was indeed magnificent, crisp-skinned, roasted to a light rose at the center, oozing juices. The peas were glossy emerald and popping fresh, the potatoes buttery, peppery. And the wine was outlandishly delicious, like a beautiful poem for the mouth, that fulfilling.

Slowly as the wine took effect they began to reminisce about Solya, about the songs she sang and the bright clothes she wore, about her effervescent laughter and her ability to listen with her whole body. They talked about how she had turned her limp into a dance, plucking sensuality from deformity.

They remembered the massive breakfasts she ate. Her abandonment to her appetite. And with her example in their minds and the wine to loosen their reservations they piled on seconds of duck and peas, applesauce and potatoes. When Goyra retrieved the platter only a handful of clean bones remained.

With the almond cream she served coffee in small cups and then, when they sprawled in their chairs imagining the meal over, she pulled from a sideboard a brandy older, she claimed, than the city they lived in. A prehistoric brandy, a brandy from the dawn of time, aged in a succession of disintegrated oaken casks in various cellars, waiting for just such a gathering.

"Are you sure you want to waste it on us?" Pico asked and she laughed. "Who else would I waste it on? This is your brandy, Pico."

A drunkenness brought on by gulped beer on an empty stomach produces raucous sniping, atrocious singing, nausea. But a tizzy induced by impeccable wine slowly sipped during a marvelous meal and burnished by a superb brandy elicits miraculous conversation. Deep into the night, as the fire congealed to coals, as the snow fell outside, they talked about secrets, the uncanny power they can release when revealed, containing energy out of all proportion to their petty atoms.

Pico put his hands up to the candelabra, holding its glow within his palms. "Solya was a candle flame," he said.

"And I'm a fire-eater who can never exhale," said Zarko morosely.

"She carried her light inside her," said Narya, "but she would not release it to everyone."

"Ah Solya," said Pico, "she knew the power of secrets. When she kissed you it was as though she took a secret from your tongue and gave you one in return."

There was sudden silence. Then Zarko slowly stood.

"What did you say?"

Pico, slightly fuddled by the wine, smiled at Zarko. "Her kisses were like secrets, I said. The shape, the secret shape two mouths make."

"You kissed her? You kissed Solya?"

"Yes, Zarko, I kissed her. We were lovers. But you had forsaken her, Zarko, you had abandoned the beautiful acrobat because of her deformity. She's dead, she's dead, let this secret escape, let it spiral through the cramped streets of this city, releasing us from our chains. Yes, I kissed her. Sit down, Zarko, sit down."

But the artist did not sit down. He lifted an arm to Pico, a finger like a hard word scrawled across the candlelight.

"Dawn," he said. "The north field. Narya will prepare the weapons." And in the awful stillness that followed they heard his boots on the flagstone floor and the rush of his cloak being swept about his shoulders and the slam of the door behind him and they felt a moment later a gelid breath from the frosty night.

The rest of that night seemed a dream. Pico was at first unsure what had come to pass. But he realized, when Narya began to describe the procedure for the duel, that Solya's tightrope had snapped, even in her absence it had snapped and he was in a free fall, uncertain whether cobbles or chrysanthemums awaited him below.

Dawn broke bright and bitterly cold. A handful of ravens arced and fell like thrown stones and then all was still in that city in the mountains, all was still save the small party that trudged through the snow, across the great bridge, Zarko leading, his strides eating the road in great bites, followed by Narya with a box under her arm. Pico brought up the rear, dawdling in this frozen prelude, as if by holding back, by brushing the snow from the ankle of a statue and picking apart a decaying leaf he could forestall the event to come. They walked out of the city with the mountains on their left, through a copse, to a field that was the setting for so many scenes in the books he'd read here. It was a frayed oval ringed by the black boles of trees, their arms splintering the sky, night lingering beneath them. On the far side of the field gravestones nudged through the snow, and in the center a spindle of knee-high black granite stood like an altar. No one spoke as they approached that marker. Narya set down the box and began making a cigarette, Pico and Zarko watching as she strewed the tobacco in the crease, curled the paper, licked and tamped it. She handed it to Zarko then made cigarettes for herself and Pico and lit them from a single match. Pico walked toward the trees and stood looking into them as if he could see something more tangible than shadows there.

Narya finished her cigarette, then she knelt and opened the box. Under the lid on rumpled satin two derringers nestled side by side like slumbering birds of prey. The guns were stocked in rosewood, trimmed with silver wire, the short barrels oiled so they shone with dark rainbows. She went to Pico and he chose a pistol and stood holding it awkwardly in both hands. Contemptuously, Zarko seized the other gun, ejected the ball and tested the mechanism. He blew down the shaft, then reinserted the bullet and flipped the pistol around his trigger finger, the haft snapping into his palm.

Narya positioned Pico and Zarko beside the spindle, then stood away to pronounce the ritual.

"When I give the command you will walk ten paces to my count, following which you are free to fire at will. Does anyone dispute these rules?"

The duelists stood motionless, back-to-back.

"Then let us begin. One. Two. Three."

Her gritty voice cast the numbers into the air where each hung a moment like a settling ash.

"Four. Five. Six."

Pico's heart stumbled and roared in his ears and then, as the numbers rose, stilled, and he felt suddenly light as though he floated above the snow watching two figures far below walk slowly away from each other, the only movement in the entire world. The spaces between the numbers seemed to sprawl into eternities.

"Seven. Eight. Nine. Ten."

His limbs felt ponderous as he turned to face Zarko. The painter had held the pistol at his ear during the paces and now he straightened and leveled his arm. Pico shook his head as if clearing his vision, looked down at the pistol and began to raise his hand.

The shot seemed very quiet, a broken twig, a finger snap, a cough. Pico was afraid he'd pulled his own trigger but then saw the fist of smoke, slowing dissipating above Zarko's gun. But the gun wasn't pointed at him and now Pico, bewildered, saw the fan of gore across the snow behind Zarko, a moment before the lanky body toppled, all at once, sideways, like a tree falling.

Pico was sick. He fell to his knees and scrubbed his face with snow as if the shock of the cold could counteract somehow the shock of the heart. He bent forward and crouched with his forehead against the ground, curled to shut out the sky, shut out the hysterical birds that circled there, until Narya came to shake his shoulder, pull at his arm.

In a changed city they sat in a cafe, the only customers, drinking coffee, and it seemed to Pico the fingertips that clutched the cup were the only parts of his body not frozen. He held to the cup as a drowning man grips the driftwood that will drag him to shore.

They sat as the cafe filled and emptied and filled again, as clouds poured over the mountains and sifted snow onto the streets. They drank coffee. They smoked. They didn't speak.

Utterly exhausted they slept that night in Pico's bed bound in each other's arms as it continued to snow. He woke once and saw that a drift on the balcony covered half the door and when he slept again he dreamed the snow had entered the room and he slumbered now beneath its blanket and a voice sang words he could not discern.

When he woke again Narya was sitting in his chair by the window wearing his coat, looking out through a space cleared in the frosted glass at the snow, thick and even on every rooftop. And still the flakes whirled down. When he sat up she turned and looked at him, then took the pouch of tobacco and packet of papers from his coat pocket and made him a cigarette.

"The body will be covered by now," she said.

"Will someone bury him?"

"In the spring, after the thaws, there will be another stone in the duelists' cemetery. Unless the ravens get there first."

"Have you lost other friends?"

She nodded.

"To duels?"

"Duels, suicide, the black house. You make your peace with these emotions or you go mad."

"Like Zarko."

"Zarko was in love. Madness, death and love are the inseparable trio in this city."

"You've never been in love, Narya?"

She pressed her hand to the window, voice so low he could hardly hear her. "At one time I thought I was in love with you, Pico, you seemed to have embraced death, setting off on a hopeless journey. But you abandoned it, you've abandoned the story that gave you power."

He said nothing.

"I've been thinking," she said, "these past hours while you slept, and I've decided to take your story from you. You discarded your story and now it is anyone's for the taking. Tomorrow I will leave, not eastward, not to your morning town. I have no wish for wings. I will retrace your footsteps west through the forest. My desire is to view the sea."

She packed a small leather portmanteau with clothes and cooking equipment and he offered her his compass.

"But what if you continue your journey?" she asked, holding the brass case with its wilful little needle under glass.

"I'll follow the sun," he replied.

The rest of that day they shopped for candles and a ball of twine, for a wedge of blue cheese, a packet of hard biscuits and a slab of smoked bacon, for a great pouch of tobacco and extra papers. She packed a dozen books and couldn't lift the case and so, while Pico stood by sympathetically, agonized over which ones to leave behind, finally settling on the three books from Pico's library and several of the slim black notebooks she wrote her own verse in.

That night they made love while the case stood in a corner of the room and then Pico slept but when he woke he was alone in bed. It had stopped snowing and the moon splashed blue light though his window. Narya sat again on his chair and he saw a single tear like a melted snowflake on her cheek.

He woke again at dawn and she had not moved though the tear was gone and he wondered if he'd dreamed it.

"Did you sleep at all?" he asked and she shook her head but her eyes were bright.

"Let's get some breakfast," she said.

They ordered enormous platters of sausages and bacon, scrambled eggs, cheese and beans, toast and fried potatoes and drank cup after cup of milky coffee and then she lifted her case and they left the steamy warmth of the cafe and went out into the snow. Along the boulevard it had been shoveled into great knolls to either side but as they moved westward through the smaller streets they slogged in knee-deep drifts. Beyond the last house they stood hand in hand looking down over the white slope that lay like a plumped eiderdown. The first trees of the forest, the firs and pines, bore fat white tails on their boughs but the distance was solid green. Narya shivered and Pico turned and put his arms around her.

"I'm not cold," she said and he smiled. "Pico," she touched his cheek, "will you attend to my manuscript? I left the door to my room open."

"Of course. I am honored. Listen, Narya. At the end of your journey when you emerge from the trees you will see the water before you lifting to the sky and the city all towers beneath you. On the slopes of the hill to your left, situated above the other houses, you will note a small ornate building of stone with copper doors and sculptures

around its walls, a cupola atop its domed roof. That is my library. The
key is beneath the doormat. You are welcome to stay there, to read the
books and sleep on the mattress in the cupola."

She faced him, eyes like stars, then kissed him and released herself
from his embrace and he watched as she trudged through the snow
down the slope toward the trees.

He had things to do. His heart strangely full he returned to the
whorehouse, descended to Narya's chamber where he smiled at the ad-
monition on the door and entered the grove of books, touching those
familiar to him. He lit the candles and sat at her desk to read the last
chapter, the chapter she must have written in the few hours between
Zarko's challenge in the restaurant and the duel at dawn, in which the
traveler returned at last to her home planet, a stranger full of stories,
where she released the starlings and set the flowerpot back in its place
and went into her mother's kitchen where her breakfast was waiting
for her.

When he had finished he bound the papers into a great bale that
he lugged up the stairs and out of the house, through the streets to the
square of booksellers. They huddled now under thick coats and blankets, though they still held pens and pencils in mittened fingers and
scribbled into their notebooks. The giant parasols sagged under bur-
dens of snow and the stone man now perused a sheaf of flakes, a
white cap on his head.

Pico set the manuscript in the lap of a startled bookseller, the

same man who had disbelieved his story when he'd first arrived in
the city.

"It's not mine," Pico said. "The author's name is Narya. She was a
whore but is now a traveler, on her way through the forest to find the
city by the sea. Read her book, it's a masterpiece, and when you're
done take it to a printer's."

The bookseller's eyes, just visible over the edge of the bale, regis-
tered astonishment. "The whore's manuscript?" he said. Pico nodded.
"Unbelievable," the bookseller gasped. "It's a legend among us booksellers that a whore was writing an extraordinary epic, we've all made
our rounds at the whorehouse, trying to bribe the girls into stealing it
for us. I guessed it was whimsy, booksellers, weary of their wares, hungry for a book that would finally satisfy. So you met her?"

"She was my friend and my lover. This book was her life."

"What can I pay you?"

"Nothing. Nothing at all. But it's important the book look beautiful. Please ensure that it looks beautiful." And Pico turned and left
the square.

He packed his knapsack now, with his notebook, two novels from
the city in the mountains, and another slim book into which he'd
copied several of the most beautiful chapters from Narya's epic.

He hefted the pack and left the whorehouse for the last time, walking through the carpeted halls with their susurrations of despair and
ecstasy. He did not leave the city alone, though his friends were dead
or gone, for at the end of the alley waited the children who had
haunted his heart. But now he smiled at them and touched their

cheeks flushed with cold, the girl with her recorder and the boy with his drum. No flower girls before them, only the two diminutive musicians to send him on his way, prescient somehow of his intentions. That tune had strayed through his veins, an acid trail of fear, but now on this dire afternoon the fear had dissipated and he heard the pure notes and beats and was glad for this small company.

He nodded to the weeping women, the stricken men who peered from doorways and windows, he touched the heads of the children who ran barefoot beside him in the snow before their mothers called them back. And then he was past the last house and the musicians stopped and turned to face him and he bent to kiss their foreheads before moving on, up the path that was no more than a vague depression in the snow. The music faded behind him as he wound among the slippery stones. Once he turned and looked at the city below, small now in the vast scree of old rockslides. The great bridge a white bow over the river, the other bridges cotton threads. He followed with his eye the streets he'd paced, picked out the cafes he'd loved and the booksellers' square, and he looked a last time at the whorehouse and the pinprick of his balcony at the top. To the right, beyond the city, was the oval clearing of the duelists' field.

From far away points converge. His months in the city contracted now to a few places he could hold in his hand, to several voices on the wind. So little, so strong. He lifted his eyes to the forest and its blue seep into sky, the forest where Narya now walked, then turned back to the slope of the mountain.

As the afternoon died a bitter wind blew up, tormenting his bones, driving ice against his skin. He pulled up his coat collar, hunched his head into it and staggered on. It seemed the sinking sun stole the oxygen from the air for as he rose it grew painful to breathe and he had to rest often that he not topple against a rock. For a long time the black facets seemed to grow no closer and certainly their mystery did not resolve but at last, under a darkling sky, amid swirling flakes, his feet met the horizontal angles of a stone stoop and he looked up and realized he'd arrived.

Seven

The Dark Castle

He'd knocked upon a number of doors on his travels but none so fearfully anticipated as this oaken slab set deep within walls of stone so black and seamless they might have been forged of iron. His knuckles shook so he had to support his wrist with his right hand. Even then the rap was so puny he wondered whether it had penetrated, but placing an ear to the boards he heard echoing footsteps. The door opened.

Expecting if not a monster at least a giant, he was taken aback to see a lad his own height, clad in black, a black hat on his head, and Pico had a notion he'd encountered the face before. A dream? His mind churned and suddenly he realized that, though the face was paler, the lips strangely scarlet, the eyes ringed in violet and sadder if possible than his own, the young man in black resembled himself. The stranger seemed not to notice the uncanny likeness and made a stiff but courteous bow and raised an open palm to bid Pico enter. The other hand held a naked rapier.

The lock snicked shut behind him. He stood in a great hall lit by basins of fire. On the floor were shreds of ancient carpet, rusting suits of armor leaned against the walls. High on the stone, almost lost in the frugal light, hung blackjacks and battle-axes, sabers and maces, bastinades and shillelaghs and pikes. Other weapons too, nameless but clearly wrought with death in mind, agony swift or slow. All were ruined now, steel pitted and tarnished, handles a lacework of wormholes, dusty cobwebs dripping from their forms.

Pico followed the stranger down the hallway, checking his pace slightly at each bowl of fire to receive a handful of heat. They turned right along another hallway, higher even than the first. Here the walls were carven into bas-relief friezes, scenes of horror, scenes of war. Shorn heads, raised scimitars, dead women raped, children spitted on spears, mouths gaped in anguish or dull death, images that coupled with the fear already palpitant within him so he had to look away that he not collapse.

At the end of that hallway stood a small door and this the stranger bent to unlock, then straightened and beckoned Pico forward. They entered a stairwell, the steps concave from countless footsteps. Up they spiraled to a tiny room at the top of a tower, slit windows facing out in three directions.

Once again his silent host bowed, then pulled the door to. Pico heard a key turn and withdraw and the echos fade.

A round room of stone, little more than two paces across, the windows just wide enough to slip a fist through. He dropped the pack and moved from one aperture to the next. In the first he saw the snow-clad slope he'd just climbed, the distant city vague under a lessening skein of flakes. The next looked into blackness crowned in stars. But the third opened over the castle and by pressing his cheekbones into the stone lips he could make out some of its architecture. He stood in the tallest of four towers that rose above an open rectangle of black roofs and walls glimmering under starlight, hulking and ominous. In the center was a courtyard that he now saw contained statues, difficult to make out from this height, hewn in crystal or alabaster, the fluid lines in utter contrast to the angular bulk of the building.

Movement in a lighted window above the courtyard drew his eye and he saw, at a long table lit with more bowls of fire, the seemingly lone tenant of this castle set a place at one end, knife, fork and goblet, then carry a salver and a flask from a sideboard. He seated himself and tucked a napkin into his collar, then removed the silver bell of the salver and served himself from a steaming joint of roasted meat. From the flask he poured a dark wine and Pico watched as he ate slowly, sipping from the goblet, never glancing around the room. Though the stranger was too distant for Pico to examine his expression nevertheless he felt a sympathetic tug in his own limbs as the other moved, like a dream in which he watched himself, so uncanny was the other's resemblance to his own body and mannerisms.

He watched till the stranger finished his meal and wiped his lips and rose to extinguish the fires. Then he sat on the floor of the chamber chafing his cheeks and forehead, which had borne the brunt of the icy wind threading the slits in the tower. He had books but no light to read so he pulled his blanket from his pack and tucked it around his knees. He slept the jerky sleep of the ill at ease. Long before sunrise it grew too cold to sit so he stood and paced, two steps forward, turn, two back, till on one swivel a wing of color brushed his eye and he realized dawn had entered the windows. He watched the flocks of ravens swirling, silent at this distance, like black dust devils over the roofs of the city, and before long he could see the awnings being raised over the cafes and wished he had some coffee. The second window looked over snow and rocks, lifeless. Now as the sun swung into the sky he could see more clearly from the third casement the sculptures in the courtyard and realized they were made of ice, light igniting the fractured interiors of the figures, transforming them into spirits, gorgeous and intricate, colorful as dewdrops.

Late in the morning the stranger, clad again in black, a black scarf swathing his throat, emerged into the courtyard. He began to chip at a block of ice as yet unformed, using his sword and a hatchet, the flakes spraying like spat milk into the air. As he moved slowly around the block the form of a struggling man emerged, shoulder here, hip there, its gestures reminiscent of something that Pico could not place. He worked an hour or two while Pico watched, then gathered his tools and went inside, the wrestler still within the ice.

The stone around the windows was dark and shiny where innumerable hands and faces had pressed and the iron door bore faint scratches as though fingernails or belt buckles had been used to pry at the metal. He set his hands and then a shoulder to the door. It was solid as the walls themselves. But the lock. He remembered the bent wire still in the bottom of his knapsack, relic from his days as a thief, and he took it out and inserted it into the keyhole. But the lock was craftily structured and he had lost the knack and it took him the entire afternoon, twiddling the implement, adjusting its angles, before the bolt clicked back.

All along as he worked at the lock he assumed he'd try to escape the dark castle if he got out of the room. But now he moved to the window overlooking the courtyard and again saw the stranger at a supper of meat and wine, the stranger with his own face and bearing, and knew he could not avoid this encounter. Awful as it was to enter into the heart of horror, his way forward included the encounter with the silent lord of this manor.

Leaving his knapsack in the room, Pico descended the stairs into the hallway of carven walls. He rounded two corners before he discovered the door in the inner wall of the far hall ringed in a wire of light. Creeping up to it, he put his ear to the keyhole and heard the clink of metal on porcelain. He turned the knob. The door was unlocked. Heart erratic, he pushed it open and entered the room.

The stranger, bent to his meal, did not notice Pico till he stopped several paces away at the edge of a circle of light. Then he looked up, dropped his utensils clattering and stared. For a long minute the two simply gazed at one another, each loath to release the hands of the clock, to tip the world into whatever precarious new architecture it might acquire.

Pico spoke first.

"I saw your sculptures from the window. They're beautiful."

The stranger rose, put a hand to a sword hilt that was not there, sat down again. He picked up his knife and fork and glanced at them dubiously.

"May I join you?" Pico asked.

The stranger jerked as if struck, then sat motionless staring at Pico who took this as a yes and pulled back a chair and sat. Scrolls of dust from the cushion set him sneezing. He blew his nose on his handkerchief and turned to his mute host whose face was so pale, lips so startlingly scarlet, eyes the sockets of a skull, though each harbored a spark as though Pico peered down two more corridors, basins of fire at their far ends.

"Well," said Pico, "you live alone here, I see."

No answer, so he continued. "I lived alone once myself, on the other side of the world." And he began to describe his library. He talked about the routine of his day in that city by the sea, waking and brewing a cup of tea, eating a heel of bread with a sliver of goat cheese on the windowsill overlooking the town and the endless water. "A view much like your own, if you care to look west," he commented. "The expanses of forest and ocean seen from a distance are not dissimilar."

Then the labor in the library, swiping the books with his ostrich-feather duster, sweeping and mopping the mosaicked floor, ensuring the titles were in order, watering the irises outside the door. The long day spent reading at his desk hoping for patrons who never arrived. The evening stroll, clutching an iris, down to the water's edge to watch his love on the wind, and then, when the wings had swept over his head, the return to the library with a bottle of milk for the cats.

Still the stranger sat, face emotionless. There was nothing to do but go on speaking and Pico had a story to tell. He told of his journey through the forest and of the creatures he'd met there, and he told of his arrival in the city in the mountains, of his encounter with Solya and the week in the dungeon, of his garret in the whorehouse.

"I had friends in the city," he said, "who loved what I loved, who worshiped beauty. Perhaps you've also had a trove of friends like this, who cherished what you did."

But the stranger only stared.

So Pico told of the destruction of that circle, of Solya's departure to this house where they now sat, of the duel and Zarko's suicide, of Narya's decision to travel to the city by the sea.

"So here I am. I said good-bye to a whore and made the journey from the city to this house to meet whatever stranger lived here and I encountered no ogre, no dragon, but a boy with my own face."

At this last revelation the knife and fork spasmed suddenly in the stranger's hands. Pico rose and placed a palm on the other's shoulder, which was cold and tense as steel.

"Come," Pico said. "Lay down your knife and fork. I want you to show me the courtyard of sculptures."

And after a moment the stranger did as he bid, rising and leading Pico out into the hallway to another door which opened onto the courtyard.

Under only starshine and the yellow wash from the dining hall windows the forms were ghostly shadows and it was difficult to discern where one figure ended and another began.

"Light," Pico exclaimed, "we need more light," and he rushed back into the hallway and carried a bowl of flame into the courtyard and set it on a windowsill. Then another and another and the stranger as well joined in the task until a dozen wells of fire circled the space.

Now the statues lived, veins of light pulsing through them. Pico moved among these figures of water and light and coldness, touching their hands, their frozen cheeks, the locks of hair like twisted icicles. The company of angels. He felt for the first time in this house a peace. No malicious fingers had whittled these features.

"They're lovely," he said, turning to the sculptor. And at last in that waxen face something stirred. Twin tears swelled in the corners of the eyes and spilled down the cheeks. Then two more.

"Who are you?" Pico whispered. "What's your name?" but the weeping sculptor shook his head.

"Tell me your name, please tell me your name," but at this the stranger put his face in his hands and at last Pico remembered what Narya had told him.

"Oh," he said, "Oh I'm so sorry. You are nameless, aren't you?" And two pairs of damp eyes identical save for the wearing of separate weathers met and clung.

Now Pico watched as the stranger lifted the bowl of fire on the windowsill nearest him and set it among the sculptures. Then the others, till the flames rose among the icy limbs, brushed the icy hair. Slowly tears began washing down the cheeks, the lines of the mouths deepening. Then the faces sloughed away completely. The forms grew etiolated, while the drip and occasional tinkle as a lock of hair or a finger fell to the ground filled the courtyard with a spring music. As the fires licked at the sculptures they grew more alike, the differences melting away till only a series of streaming glossy cones stood among the hot bowls, like the aftermath of some indecipherable ritual.

At last the stranger, turning to Pico, spoke. "Come in," he said, his voice strange to Pico's ears, for our own voices are unfamiliar to us. "Come in, I'm hungry and you interrupted my dinner."

So Pico followed the nameless sculptor back into the dining hall where he hoped his host would share the repast for he had not eaten now for a night and a day. And indeed the sculptor fetched another place setting from a sideboard as Pico looked hungrily at the meat on the salver, a slender joint basted brown, in a moat of thick juice. But as the ivory-handled knife and fork sank into the flesh he realized, with a shock that shoved a scream up his throat and choked it back halfway to his lips, the roasted meat was a human forearm. He could see the curled fingers, flesh peeling from the bone, the exposed knuckles glistening umber, the fingernails cracked and darkened. Part of the arm had been cut away, already eaten, and now the sculptor eagerly carved off another chunk, the meat beside the bone pinkish, oozing blood.

"Oh I can't," Pico managed as the sculptor was about to slide the meat onto his plate. And added, "I'm sorry," concerned he'd offended his host.

"No," the sculptor said. "I understand. One forgets the taboos. After so long, so long."

"How long?"

"Since I have supped with someone, since I have spoken with someone? A century perhaps, perhaps more. I do not chart the years in this house."

"I'm afraid I misheard," Pico said. "I thought you said you'd been silent a century."

"Much longer probably."

"But you're no older than I am."

"Oh certainly I am. Much older. I'm the oldest you see."

"I don't understand."

"The houses of the city below us are all new to me, they are built on foundations of houses razed in my youth. The large bridge over the river was erected during my lifetime. I am older than the ancient chestnuts that line the boulevard."

"Then what are you? Are you not human? Are you immortal?"

"Is my story no longer told in the city?"

"I've heard only rumors."

"Yes," his scarlet lips curled slightly at the corners. "The memories of the doomed are short and veer quickly into myth. So you know nothing of my story?"

"Tell me."

During the telling, oblivious to Pico's horror, or perhaps aware but immunized against silent opprobrium by centuries of disgust, the sculptor devoured his meal, paring the meat from the twin bones of the forearm, then pulling off the fingers and sucking them clean, spitting the nails onto the plate.

"I come from an ancient tribe," he said, "of which I am the sole survivor. We were, as you have discerned, a tribe of immortals, destined to survive forever as long as we could ensure a supply of the food that kept us young," and he held up a finger bone. "Human flesh. No other victual has entered my lips, and no liquid other than human blood, since my birth thousands of years ago.

"I did not always live apart. No, once I dwelt with my relatives in the heart of the city, in a palace many of whose stones now form this castle. You may imagine us a race of malign cannibals wallowing in depravity but it was not so, for we possessed a gentility surpassing that of common folk. Our sopranos gave recitals in our ballrooms, we staged elaborate pageants for our own pleasure, our writers and artists produced works of great poignancy, and though we ate human flesh we ate it off fine porcelain and drank the blood that was our wine from cut crystal. At dusk we promenaded arm in arm down the boulevard, deserted at that hour, past drawn curtains and whispers. Forever young, forever famished. Can you imagine our lives, the constant desire for flesh, the weariness with the company we kept? We'd long forgotten laughter. In the ancient halls of our palace drapes rotted in the windows, tapestries decayed on the walls. The forlorn power over the common folk, our prey. Can you imagine our lives, I ask, but never once during those centuries did it occur to me to place myself in their skins, in their mortal skulls which I would shortly cleave to spoon out tender brains. Not till much later did I try to imagine a life which did not linger through the years but which would certainly, after a few short days, be snuffed like a candle.

"And don't imagine I was not tempted by your pastries and sauces, by the aroma of fresh bread and the tang of apples. They are as appetizing to me as they are to you, and this fate of mine at times as repugnant. But it was only this that gave us our endless years, that we had never, since we emerged from the womb, allowed any morsel past our lips that was not of our own flesh and blood. The human sustained us, anything other was our doom.

"What to do with the hours when one's life is eternity? Some wrote, filling ream upon ream with words that would die before they did. Others gardened, enamored of the small cycles that sustained the world beyond our immortal skins, the finger-snap existences of butterflies and flowers. Even trees did not outlive us. I have witnessed the diminishing of mountains.

"I chose to embrace the permanent. Stone, those bones of the earth, born in fire, heaved through a skin of soil, whose lifetimes may not be measured in the generations of humans but in the cycles of dynasties, whose shapes are only altered by the great powers, wind and heat and water. And human hands. The black rock of these mountains is more durable than iron, more durable perhaps than the human spirit. I sought among the rockslides, the flotsam of the mountains' ponderous restlessness, chunks of unflawed stone. And I had these boulders dragged on log rollers to the space below my window for no studio could have admitted their bulk. Working on wooden scaffolds, the ground thick with black flakes, I carved the statues that now adorn the great bridge."

Pico gasped. "Those are yours?"

"They are the labor of centuries, so ancient that none in the city now remembers the hands that crafted them."

"They're beautiful. My first night in the city I knew no one and I made my bed at the base of one of those statues, laid my head upon a great ankle and that enormous presence comforted me."

"I can see them from here, sometimes I look down upon their forms, too distant to make out clearly, though of course I know every curve by heart."

"Did you make the sculpture of the reading man?"

"The reading man? Ah yes, to honor a poet, not one of our tribe but a mortal, who had nevertheless contrived words that expressed the loneliness of immortality. I loved to read poetry. I had shelfloads here once, but they long ago disintegrated.

"Anyway you can see the gap, the trough of ages between the time when my family paced the cobbles of the boulevard at dusk and the present when I am the lonely lord of a bleak castle in the snows.

"Our appetite was our downfall, our appetite and our breeding, the slow but inexorable swelling of our numbers. And whereas in the early days of our dynasty we could easily cull the pariahs of the city, the prisoners, the sick and the lame, and be satisfied, indeed perform a service, keeping the race of humans unadulterated, now as the family grew immense we were forced to enter houses and turn them into abattoirs, whole families slaughtered for a single supper.

"Of course under this duress the city folk rose against us. They poured from their houses one day with their puny weapons, pitchforks and knitting needles, pruning hooks and sickles, and made war upon us, besieging us in our palace, shouting that this time we would be their dinners.

"Naturally they lost the battle, they had no experience in bloodletting, whereas we had honed our blades for centuries. Though they outnumbered us we mowed them down like so much sweet hay and gore ran in the gutters. They lost the battle, I said, but they won the war. For of course though we feasted for a week the bodies of the slain soon rotted and we realized we'd cut our own feet from under us, we had destroyed the source of our nourishment.

"For a month or two we were able to round up stragglers, those who had barricaded themselves in their houses or fled to the surrounding fields. But slowly we began to starve.

"One by one my relatives succumbed to the temptation of ordinary food, relinquishing immortality for a raspberry tart or a slice of buttered toast, and just as quickly they were devoured in turn by those of us still obdurate in our creed. At last only two remained, I and my lover, a cousin of frail bones but powerful will. The loneliest of all our race. We made a pact to starve before we relinquished our tradition. And starve we did, our ribs jutting like bare cupboard shelves, our knees and elbows knots in the strings of our limbs. We boiled and re-boiled the bones of our relatives, the broth growing ever thinner. But then came a night when I woke and found the sheets empty beside me and far away in the house I heard a noise that I took for rats but when I investigated I discovered my lover crouched in the corner of the kitchen nibbling a bread crust.

"My hunger and anger, and my grief, overwhelmed me, and catching up a cleaver I hacked away her head.

"The next years were arduous. I packed my lover's body in ice, sampled her flesh slowly, eating first the eyeballs, the brain, the delicious breasts, then the scant meat of her arms and legs, and lastly boiling the bones, cracking them to release the marrow. Thus I survived, gaining strength to scour the town and uncover a number of citizens cowering in attics or cellars with hoarded food, children locked into chests beneath beds, grandmothers stashed like old lumber in ceilings. Of these I chose a young boy and girl, brother and sister, to start a new generation. Every shopkeeper, fire-eater, cobbler, chandler, flautist and thief in the city are descendants of those two plucked from the ruins how many millennia ago. Their compatriots kept me alive long enough for them to breed, then I rationed myself until I had several breeding couples that could supply me with every other child.

"A long time I lived in the city as the population slowly swelled and when the streets were lively in the evenings once more I called the city leaders to me and proposed a plan. The citizens would help me dismantle the palace and build a castle in this col where we now sit, a mansion for a single soul. I assured them I would not descend to stalk the streets at midnight seeking flesh, if they would send me one of their number each month. And thus it has continued for centuries. Every few weeks I hear a knock at the door and open it to find a pale-faced lad or quivering maiden and I welcome them and lead them to the kitchen if I'm hungry or up to the tower chamber to wait until I am. I was surprised at your knock yesterday evening as I'd only started on my last offering a few days ago, a young girl with beautiful hair."

"Solya."

"You knew her? She's very tender."

"Didn't you talk with her? Didn't you ask her name?"

"It is not my wont to fraternize with my dinners."

"What are we doing?"

"You are the first to escape the tower. How did you accomplish it, if I may ask?"

Pico showed him the lockpick. "I was once a thief."

"And can you fight as well?"

"I never have, though I learned the techniques from a woman whose passion was fighting."

"What are we going to do?" The nameless lord regarded Pico with expressionless eyes.

Pico looked at him, prying with his gaze into that blank face. "Why do you no longer carve in stone?" he asked.

"Ah. Ice. Such a beautiful medium, the interior and exterior in tension and harmony. I have become in my solitary years enamored of evanescence. I no longer desire to create durable monuments. Living alone with my memories, I have come to believe that beauty is something which may not be captured but is fleeting as a snowflake. How many snowflakes have I known? How many do I recall? I remember only one, the first flake of the first snowfall of some long-ago winter which landed on my lover's cheek, burned a moment like a star, then was a tear brushed away. The world is filled with such snowflakes, scarred into time, into memory. There is, if you know how to look, a sparkling in the darkest corners, the residue of lost gestures made in that place. So I sculpt in ice, hoping to let these forms free somehow into the atmosphere when the sun diminishes them."

"I've wondered," said Pico, "where the poems that escape my pen wander to. When I lie down at night words sweep my sleep, reaping my dreams so I wake with poems spilling from my tongue, poems that hum into the morning like bumblebees and I snatch at them, missing most, mutilating some. Where do the uncaught poems fly to? Do they suckle in distant ears, pollinating as they go? Or perhaps you are right that they remain in the air where someone else can snag them. Perhaps my poems are words I've blundered into unwittingly, hung like ornaments from the boughs of breezes. Perhaps they are not numberless but passed around, and we can each make our honey from them if we brave the stings."

And Pico recited for the lord of the dark castle:

"The sun is falling into the trees,
the day is falling into dusk
as the sky tells its beads of birds.
These rocks are fallen,
the river is falling from the sky,
the river which has been glaciers
and bears last year's leaves
and the shadows of ravens.
The river is falling into the forest
and the leaves are falling, falling to the earth
and the earth is falling into the stars."

"It's been ages since I sat by the river," the sculptor said. "I loved its voice, fleeting and eternal."

"Why do you fear death?"

"Don't you?"

"On this journey I've become enamored of mystery. The steps into the dark, terrifying and wonderful. This is what a thief taught me, to pick locks and revere mystery. How can you know you love if you lack that unopened door at the end of your life?"

"I am hungry, I sleep, I create."

"But do you love?"

"I ate my love."

"You didn't love her. Only in retrospect, now that she's become circle rather than arrow, can you guess what it might have been to love her."

"Who are you to tell me, I who am ancient, what I feel?" But though the sculptor's words held rancor his face bore no frown, no tensed lip.

"I am in love," Pico smiled. "I can sense its lack or presence in others."

The sculptor looked down. "What does it feel like?" he whispered.

"To be in love for an hour," Pico replied, "is worth the weight of a hundred years lacking it. Slay me now and my love would haunt this house, cooing like doves in the eaves, shrieking like bats in the rafters."

"But I'm afraid."

"You've been wandering in the cold, alone, but only an hour's walk away the vendors along the boulevard are setting up their stalls, frying bean cakes, tumbling strawberries into paper cones, brewing coffee and cocoa. Laughter, children crying, couples squabbling, kisses. Bookshelves filled with volumes of poetry. You have years of love ahead of you, years."

"And at the end nothing."

"Death. Yes. Death, which is worth a single kiss."

"A single kiss." The sculptor rose suddenly and Pico noted a faint fanning of color through his cheeks, an unclenching of the spark in the center of each eye as though a caged bird gingerly splayed maimed wings.

They joined hands and walked through the halls, fists passing briefly through the coils of heat above each bowl of fire.

Then, trembling even as Pico had when entering the great door, the sculptor bent to unlock it. He flung it open onto a night clear as water, bright with fallen snow, the city glittering below. He spread his arms then drew them abruptly to his chest and turned to Pico, his voice small.

"But I can't go down there," he said. "I have forgotten my name. I can't go among people nameless."

Pico laughed. "Use mine," he said. "Pico is your name." And he gave the other a nudge between the shoulder blades to start him on his way, the first footsteps in millennia to face the city, footsteps that would release the city in the mountains from its terrible shackles.

Alone in a castle lit by bowls of fire he was suddenly faint with hunger. His evocation for the sculptor of the delicacies being served along the boulevard nearly drove him delirious, but he could not retrace his journey. And in this frozen waste was no food save one. He stumbled to the scullery beside the dining hall. It was spotless, pans of all sizes hanging from nails, a cast-iron stove against one wall. He entered the cold-storage pantry with its vents to admit the wintry weather. And here from hooks hung Solya's dismembered body. The sight of the limbs and breasts he'd so recently seen warm and supple forced him to his knees and he pressed his cheek against the cold wall, whimpering. But hunger will always override taboos. Besides, he'd already known appetite toward this body. Had he not nibbled and licked at her flesh, probed with his tongue to lap the juices? Even her blood he'd tasted. His teeth had already entered her skin. Trembling, he chose a haunch, the curved flesh he'd loved to lay his hand upon, lifted it from an iron prong and carried it into the kitchen.

Now, as if back in Goyra's kitchen, he kept close watch on the meat, turning it as it browned in the oven, the kitchen filling with the marvelous aroma of grilling fat. When the juices ran clear under his fork prick he carried the roast to the table, saliva pooling like honey under his tongue. Only a moment did he hesitate before lifting the first morsel to his lips and then the ecstasy of eating bore all nausea away. She was delicious.

After his meal he wandered through the hallways till he discovered the sculptor's bedroom, dark curtains slung about a four-poster, the discarded rapier hanging in its scabbard from a finial. He crept between sable sheets and slept.

Late in the morning he woke and fetched his knapsack from the tower. As there was no door in the eastern wall of the castle he slipped through a window onto the roof and sat on the snow-clad tiles taking in the view, his first glimpse of the country to come. He saw that the castle was situated at the highest point of a pass. On either side peaks rose, icily inscrutable. But below him the land tumbled away, the facets of rock and ice mellowed sporadically by pockets of snow. Farther down the angles abraded into ridges and then the softer shapes of foothills. And beyond those hills were azure gulfs that might contain any geography but had acquired the aspect of sky.

Height had always exhilarated him, he'd lived in a cupola and a garret, but now he straddled the world. Perched on this lofty meridian he was surrounded by more space than he'd dreamed existed. The city in the mountains with its close-set walls and unceasing rain and fog, bound by a long terror, had built a silver cage around his skull, had knotted a silk scarf across his eyes. Now his emotions poured into all this air that was hungry for them and he felt he was adequate to fill this space, he had within him enough celebration, enough shout, to top these vaults. The sculptor had named the human spirit as one of the few powers that could tame rock and he thought as he sat in this place, twirling on the axis of the earth, that his spirit could take on the sky, the stars, as well. A long time he reveled in this giddy euphoria while the snow slid like pale eels down the roof and fell with gentle thuds from the eaves and finally he decided it was time he followed. He inched down the tiles. At the edge he stuck a foot in the gutter and peered over and muttered a prayer of relief that he hadn't slipped for far below like waiting sharks' teeth lurked blades of rocks. He moved along the ledge till he was above a snowdrift and flung out the pack, which sank soundlessly from sight. Then he eased over backward, clung to the lip of the gutter, swung out and released his grip, pleading silently that no black shard awaited him beneath the smooth surface.

The landing was a smack by a pillow. Chin-deep in powder snow he shook his head like a dog, laughed, then floundered out and gathered his pack from the burrow it had delved. He looked back at the castle, even more imposing from this side as no windows opened eastward. And there was no possibility of return, so smooth the walls, so steep the surrounding crags. Turning into the winter landscape he began to negotiate his way forward, downward.

At noon he left the last snow behind, grateful, for his eyes had begun to smart from the glare, and toward evening he came among the first bushes and stunted trees. Searching a campsite, he scared a grouse from a nest cunningly snuggled between two rocks. She had sat four eggs, of which he took three, leaving a single dappled oval for her to incubate. He found a campsite well away from her cradle, gathered twigs and made a fire, then boiled the eggs in water doled from his bottle.

Though he'd eaten outdoors in the city in the mountains, he'd forgotten the pleasure of eating a meal procured and cooked himself. The egg he savored this evening, small birds veering about with thin cries, a darkening chasm of unknown landscape below him, rivaled any cafe feast in the city in the mountains.

The sunset percolated all through the atmosphere so he felt he sat within a gemstone, smoky topaz or flawed amber. Not the sign of another soul had he seen since he left the castle, not a footprint or trail or spear of smoke. In the forest, though he was often alone, yet there was always the possibility that beyond those trees a doorway awaited him, or a path or another traveler. Here he was certain in his solitude and this provided peace. Now words came, as he sat before his twig fire, and he leaned his notebook to the frail light, the only luminescence in that vast night save the high stars which perhaps were campfires of other travelers on their errands above. Scribing likewise into notebooks their own stellar reveries. He glanced up and saluted them, figments or no, then bent back to the page. Memories must enter the bloodstream, must churn awhile through the heart's mill, must be crushed and polished, be nearly forgotten or cling like burrs to other stories before they spill forth in purple patterns, shapes of small bones and worm rot, shapes of clouds and the spaces between leaves. In the cupola of his library he'd transcribed his dreams. In the forest he'd written of the sea and wings. Here on a rocky hillside he jotted evocations of shadows and rustlings and undergrowth.

Eight

The Valleys of the Country of Death

Three days Pico walked across the lowering waves of foothills through ever-sparser vegetation till one afternoon he stood on a slope which descended without undulation to a vast flayed lion's hide, an unbroken beach, a tawny ocean. A few trees speckled the plain before him, caught in scanty nets of shade. And far out like pale fossil whales several dunes reared, sleek and lovely, the color, he thought, of Sisi's skin. He sat and took off the pack and looked out to the horizon. He had no food. Where would he find water? It seemed the very country of death. A long time he sat, stunned by the immensity of the wasteland before him.

He needed water first, so he walked southward, parallel to the desert, till he came upon a narrow brook that skimble-skambled over rocks, then pooled in a small green-fringed bowl before spilling over the lip, into the desert. He took off his clothes and submerged himself in that coolness, lying back with only his face above the water, eye-ing the hawks which eddied in the blue. He spent that night at the edge of the desert and in the morning filled his water bottle and de-scended into the dry land alongside a sliver of green.

For an hour he followed the stream until it foundered in a small marsh ringed by acacias where he was able to fell a duck. He plucked and gutted the bird and grilled it for his lunch. Already it was hot. Glazed in sweat, he napped beneath a tree, waking under a raucous membrane of flies. Upstream he drank till his stomach sloshed, then filled the water bottle, adjusted the pack and walked on past the marsh into the vacant country beyond.

A forest is mystery but the desert is truth. Life pared to the bone. The landscape honed, softness long ago devoured so the only rest for the eye is on the haunch of a dune, the haze of the horizon, one's own shadow. In a grain of sand is the desert distilled. Immutable, adamant, without ulterior meaning. A grain of sand. Like a morsel of the soul, bleached to its essence by wind and sun.

He passed the last of the acacias and set out among the dunes, he and the sun pacing in opposite directions. And though it seemed he moved more rapidly than the white eye above yet it reached its desti-nation before he reached his for the horizon was still as distant as ever, and as blank, by sundown. Terrifyingly tiny in that country, he walked well into the night, the only sounds those he made, his tattered breath and the shuffle of his soles on the sand. The moon rose like a pale bark in a dry riverbed and when it stood above him he halted, drank a mouthful of water and slept in a sandy trough.

He woke chilled and sore. The moon was capsizing over the mountains and the stars bobbled in its wake. Eastward an opal node lay on the horizon. He drank a little water and set off toward that blemish in the dark. How rapidly the night cool evaporated. Before the sun had spanned a quarter of the sky the heat smote from the sand so he staggered, eyes slitted, an arm out to block the glare. He was in an ocean of fire, in the terrible pastures of light.

He looked back along the way he'd come, the mountains now smoothed to torn blue paper, their foothills minor discolorations like the random pooling of paint in watercolors. He did not look back again.

Each dune was a cliff. His footsteps spawned avalanches, his boots filled with sand. It was like wading through mud, and always another dune rose before him, bulwark not the less formidable for being transient.

But he was not immune to the beauty. The wind, working with such a malleable medium, achieved perfection. Dunes like wrinkled eyelids, like old tusks, like scattered sliced fruit, muskmelon or mango, their sides scalloped like nets, like concave fish scales, no two shapes identical. There is no monotony in the desert. Within the strictures of the palette is an infinite variety of hue.

Shadows shriveled as the sun neared its meridian, his own a paltry clot squirming between his legs as though in agony from the scalding surface it traversed. He came upon bones in the sand, ribs like long fangs agape at the sky, that he stared at dully a moment. Then he drew the blanket from his pack and stretched it across them, a makeshift awning he crawled beneath. Blessed shade. He drank, felt the water soak instantly into his marrow, and it took an effort not to empty the bottle onto his parched tongue. He shook the container, that diminishing slosh his only weapon against this terrain, and grimacing placed it back in the knapsack.

He woke with a headache. It was cooler. He crawled from his shelter into the wider shelter of a dune's shadow, the sun tipped below its edge. He packed the blanket and set off once more. Night descended like a benediction and still he trudged, mindless, every effort of his brain expended in shifting his limbs, till he could move no more and sank into the erasure of sleep.

Next day he passed out of the dunes and into a landscape of stones. Easier going, though he had to take care not to turn an ankle. He built cairns to support his blanket at noon, then walked again as the shadows lengthened. Now for the first time he could taste death. It was the taste of a stone. Death awaited him in this desert like a companion he had yet to meet. There is no water in the country of death, there live only those who can drink the light and eat the stones and there are none who can drink the light, none who can eat the stones.

He beat back these thoughts with his fists, shouted hoarsely against them, his voice a rustle of sand grains. He struggled on.

At dusk of that day he arrived at a well, a simple stone circle in a field of sand, a single palm tree beside it. There was no bucket so he pulled his tin pot from his pouch, tied a length of twine to the wire handle and lowered it, the faint splash it made like the voice of a lover to his ears. It was the most delicious liquid he'd ever tasted, light as air, strong as rum. He drank again, ate some dates off the tree, then spread his blanket beside the well and slept.

Deep in the night he woke beneath a lopsided moon and saw sitting on the lip of the well a woman, beautiful and sorrowful, wearing a torn singlet once white, feet bare, hair like a tattered banner fallen across her shoulders.

"Sir," she said, "by your kindness would you draw me some water? I have traveled far and am thirsty."

"Certainly," replied the poet and he filled his makeshift pail, from which she sipped slowly, eyes on his. When she finished drinking she handed the pot back and began to weep.

"Oh beautiful lady, don't cry," said Pico. "Tell me your sorrows."

"I apologize," she murmured and touched away the tears with her fingertips. "Yours is the first act of kindness anyone has paid me for ever so long." She turned to him and patted the stone and he sat beside her on the lip of the well.

"Sir," she said, "we have not properly introduced ourselves. My name is Aia." Her hand in his was cool as the well water.

"I am Pico."

"And how did you come to this well in the middle of a desert where so few travelers wend their way?"

So he told his story, of his love for Sisi, his desire for wings and the letter that had spurred him on this journey, of the hindrances and assistances he had encountered and of the morning town that he struggled toward. She sighed often during the telling, sighing seemed her nature. She was thin, her eyes huge, hooped in shadow, and she impressed him as unbearably weary, as one who had arrived through untellable trials and was not at ease with her forward way.

"Ah," she said when he was done, "the vagaries of love, we are all vagabonds in the badlands of the heart."

"Are you in love as well?" Pico asked, though he knew the answer before she spoke.

"Yes, I am in love, I love." She drew her palms over her cheeks, clasped them at her breast.

"Tell me your story."

"Listen," she said. "Far to the south the desert ends in a city of flowers and there I grew up the vainest creature in all the world. You called me beautiful but certainly I am hideous compared with my loveliness as a child, as a damsel. My skin pure as milk, eyes limpid as those of lambs, the color, as you see, of the sky at dusk. My lips delectable as candied rose petal, voluptuous as velvet. My breasts, ah my breasts were legends in their time, soft as rotting pears, the nipples purple as plums. Even as a child my walk fueled men's fevers, nightly salted their sheets with inadvertent white filth. Despite the curses of their wives they gasped as I passed in the streets and gnawed their own forearms to keep from screaming. Painters squandered their savings to sketch me fully clothed, poets and musicians camped outside my window hoping to glimpse a star of flesh through a crack in the curtains, dreaming that a note of theirs, or a phrase, might one day catch my fancy, merit my glance.

"In my city beauty is celebrated above all else. Flowers in every window, bordering every street. The houses are painted blue and yellow and green and pink and even the roofs are patterned, the tiles made from colored clays. Stained glass in the windows. Bushes are snipped into fanciful topiary. Singing insects in tiny cages of split and gilded bamboo are fed on nougat and command extraordinary prices in the markets.

"My parents were delighted to have engendered in this city of the visual the most exquisite vision of all. Some might have cloistered such a child, penned her in an attic with books in order that she develop an interior life to match her outlandish exterior, but I was given a room whose walls were mirrors and slobbering tailors were invited to make clothes to match my looks, gowns of taffeta, gowns of organdy. Hairdressers fought for the right to shape my locks. A hundred times a day I listened to exclamations over my beauty and I could only believe them for the mirrors told the same story, with equal sincerity. Often I stood before the glass walls of my room, naked or clothed, for meditating upon beauty was much encouraged.

"As I came of age there was a spate of divorces in the city as men shed their wives in order to better their chances of attracting me. But though I flirted with every male from blushing adolescent to arthritic grandfather I let not one place a hand upon my body. So, like an egg, replete in my own perfection, I became the object of a cult, the idol of a warped religion.

"How tormented are we the beautiful, for when our beauty fades, when our skin shrivels and our breasts cast their eyes to the ground, we are dead while those who have spent their ugly adolescences in the pursuit of knowledge or passion will be sustained into old age. And because none can ever compare to what we are, we are forever searching. In my room of mirrors I lost my heart and in its place built a box of silvered glass secretly echoing itself.

"Now among my admirers was a young florist remarkable as far as I could tell only for his extraordinary ugliness. He was skinny as a hatstand, the vertebrae like knuckles in his neck. His nose was a weapon, blunt and enormous, an ill-carven club, his mouth off-center, his eyes bulbous as an insect's. He walked with his feet aimed inward as if to greet each other, head sagging on a scrawny stalk, though his eyes peered about uncannily alert as though some other being used his body as its mode of transportation.

"He pushed his painted cart with its striped awning through the streets ringing a small bell and housewives would open their doors and call him over, to choose a dozen roses or a bunch of lilies for the vases on their mantels. Other florists paced the streets but this lad had a knack for providing fresh flowers out of season, for procuring rare blooms on demand, and he made a good business. He lived on the outskirts of the city with his uncle, who had been the chief gardener of the city but was now a penniless drunkard swiping the boy's earnings to buy his whisky. His nephew had inherited his knack for horticulture, however, and cultivated his flowers around the house. He was often in trouble with the authorities for his beds were not ordered according to tradition. His garden was chaos, a tempest of color, and weeds were allowed to grow among the flowers he raised for sale. Often in the evenings he could be seen among the weeds with shears and trowel, carefully pruning. It was bruited he was mad but his flowers were the finest, the freshest, so his quirks were tolerated.

"Every afternoon I strolled through the streets beneath my parasol surrounded by girls concealing their jealousy under simpers. Men if they are envious distance themselves from their rivals or fight them, but women fawn over their beautiful companions, while honing their blades for private gossip. And one day as we so promenaded the ungainly florist parked his cart across our path and refused to budge until I had spoken with him.

"'Oh what do you want?' I cried petulantly for my progress through the city was endlessly hampered by such male impositions and it was a symptom of my pride that I feigned annoyance, though these intrusions were the salt of my excursions.

"Stuttering and blushing, unable to meet my eye, he begged to be allowed to arrange the flowers in my room. At no expense to me, he'd provide the plants, he only desired the opportunity to make my chamber beautiful.

"Now the only objects that could vie with my face for my attention were flowers, those delicate genitals, always flawless, romance made tangible. I never had to buy them as the bouquets of admirers always filled my vase. My weakness was well known. The ugly florist's suggestion appealed to me greatly for he was known as a master of the bouquet but I said only that he should talk with my parents and I gave the cart a shove that sent him running after it, feet slapping like the flight of pigeons.

"He arrived that very evening bearing an armful of blooms and I watched as he knelt before the vase crafting an arrangement of extraordinary delicacy, spare, asymmetrical though perfectly balanced, using corroded angular branches and sprigs of dry thorn to set off the orchids and daffodils, never overwhelming the arrangement with a cacophony of color but allowing each petal to speak for itself. He was an artist, totally absorbed in his work, adjusting a twig fifty times before he was satisfied.

"Later he crafted arrangements more audacious, vases full of wildflowers or dried cattails. Or grass. We never look at the grass, though it is ubiquitous. If it's left alone to shake its hair loose it will produce tiny tassels and flowers, miniature and beautiful, that I'd never noticed before. Beauty is so often size and commotion for us, and fancy labels, that the subterfuge of loveliness all around us goes unseen.

"I got in the habit of serving him tea and cakes, preparing a more elaborate feast each time, and we would converse about many subjects but mostly discussed our mutual passion. At first I scoffed at his knowledge, he was so easy to taunt. He never retorted but would accept the insult solemnly and, when I was done, continue where he'd left off.

"He knew the name of every flower and its season and how it might be cultivated. He spoke of flowers as one speaks of friends and told me his theories of flower arranging, a credo celebrating nature, endeavoring to erode the artifice about conventional arranging. Slowly I left off insulting him and became enamored of his world, of the motions of his thoughts. He wept when he told me how the wildflowers were neglected. 'Nobody sees them,' he sobbed. 'They are orphans, waifs, banished to empty lots and ditches. Does one love a flower less because its name is forgotten?'

discovered his uncle propped bleary-eyed in a doorway and asked him where his nephew had gone but he was unable to tell me.

"Thirteen months after his departure, on the longest night of the year, I was woken by a kiss. My first kiss and my last, fresh as acacia blossom, fleeting as the flying ant's flight. My heart caroming around my ribs, I sat up and reached for my lover but grasped only the night breeze. Opening my eyes I saw that the vase on the windowsill that had stood empty for over a year now bore a single bloom, pale and round and shining, its scent sweet as honey but with a note of decay. Shaking like wind chimes, I walked to the flower, bent my face to its strange light and breathed in the perfume of a corpse, brought to me from another world by an unseen hand, and as I entered that scent I received a vision, as if the flower were a window I peered into. I saw the valley from which this flower had come, a dry gulch ringed by crags, and in that parched basin, rooted in dust, fed by no water, blessed by no sun, stood three pale flowers on pale stalks. And as I watched a hand reached from the shadows, a hand from which all flesh had sloughed away, a hand of bones, and it plucked a flower with a hollow snap, the sound of a pebble dropped into a dry well, and withdrew from my sight.

"Then I knew the cost to my love of the gift I had desired. I brought my hands to the flower to lift it to my face but the instant my fingertips touched the petals they crumbled to a pinch of ash in the bottom of the vase, the cloying scent lingering in the room. A flower from the country of death may not be touched by living hands and survive. And as I discovered, the living as well must pay a price.

"You may imagine the horror that seized me. I screamed, gagging,

"He took me to his house one evening, to his garden of weeds, and bade me look into the jungle there. And though from afar the yard looked as chaotic as a glade in the woods, when I knelt among the stems I saw that it was carefully ordered according to his quirky notions, not in rows and banks, not ordered as numbers are ordered, but according to the off-kilter rhythms of the heart, the electricity that branches like small lightnings through our skulls.

"But now I became the recipient of insults. My parents and friends, noticing the time I spent with the florist, shouted that I had fallen in love with a weed, that I had lost my virtue, that all my effusions about beauty were so much drivel if I could sully my reputation by befriending an ogre.

"So I spurned him. I joked with my friends about his vulturous hunch, his battering ram of a nose, I called him names in the street and if I passed his cart pulled the flowers from their basins and hurled them to the cobbles and trampled them. And finally under this barrage he ceased coming to me in the evenings though he would still wheel his cart by the house and halt a little apart from the other admirers and gaze up at my room. I would snuff the candles that I might peer out from the curtains unnoticed and my tears fell into my jasmine tea for I had not known I loved him till he left me. Till I forced him to leave me. Over and over I recited the conversations we'd had, those conversations that set me free from the confines of mirrors. There had been no need to preen or pose in his presence for I had not considered him worthy of my attentions and thus he'd circumvented my pride.

"What is precious is beautiful. Others had called him a weed but they were the weeds, striving for uniformity and thus achieving dull-ness, anonymity. He stood alone like a single amaryllis in a mown lawn pouring off beauty as a volcano spews lava. If only I had been able to articulate that sentiment then as I am able to now. But my pride had locked him out, and locked me in, and I had lost the key.

"Desperately I scoured my brain for a ruse that might bring him back and yet keep my pride intact. I remembered at last an old con-versation. I had asked him about the rarest flowers and he'd told me of a certain desert flower the size of a moth that blooms once in fourteen years and of a flower of the snows that opens its petals for only a minute before it is devoured by frost and of the carnivorous flower of the deep forest that thrives on bats and lizards and has green fanged jaws that might strip a toe off an unsuspecting traveler. He told me of the flower the size of a barrel that stinks like fetid meat and of the tiny treetop flower shaped like a wasp and of the flowering vine whose stamens produce a perfume, an ounce of which costs the price of a house.

"'And have you seen all these?' I asked and he assured me he had for his life had been spent searching such blooms.

"'But which of them,' I asked, 'which of the flowers is the rarest? Is there one so rare even you have not come across it?'

"Then he was silent and sat bent over his cup of tea which he held in his fingertips as if afraid of bruising it. Finally he looked up.

"'There is one flower,' he said, 'which my uncle told me of, a frag-ment of horticulturists' lore, which neither he nor I nor any gardener alive has ever seen.'

"'And which flower is that?'

"'It is the flower that grows in the valleys of the country of

"And he would say no more though I pleaded to know wha flower looked like, what its scent was. He set down his tea and s his head and left to wheel his cart back to his shack.

"I remembered this conversation and at last devised a plan. next afternoon as I walked with my girlfriends we heard his bell in distance and I herded my flock toward his cart. When we reached i stopped and turned to him, placed a hand on the wooden haft he hel

"'Flower boy,' I said, 'would you like to kiss me?'

"My girlfriends cackled knowing this for mockery. When he had first approached me he had stammered and rouged like a maiden but now he raised his wretched face and looked into my eyes and said sim-ply, 'Yes.'

"'Then,' I said, 'you must bring me a flower, for my vase is empty. But I am no ordinary girl and no ordinary flower will do. You must bring me the rarest flower of all, the flower that grows in the valleys of the country of death.'

"At that he turned very pale, though his eyes stayed on my face. A long time we stared at one another in silence and all merriment evap-orated from the gaggle of girls behind me. Even they sensed the power behind my words.

"At last he nodded and in a voice barely above a whisper said, 'I will bring it.' And he wheeled his cart past me and down the street to his home.

"Then he disappeared. For a year I did not see him and the house-wives lamented for the quality of their bouquets had plummeted and they could no longer purchase the exotic blooms they desired. Once I calling his name, but only my parents rushed in. They tried to quiet me, saying I had been visited by a nightmare, but I would not hush. I threw myself about the room shattering the mirrors and tried to cast myself from the window so they tied me to the bed with torn sheets and bathed my face as if I were feverish. Perhaps I was. I remember little of the next weeks.

"I recall only waking up one day, calmer though no less tormented, with a certainty of what I must do. My parents, hearing my sane though weak voice, released me from my bonds and brought me broth and sweet tea and let me rest in the darkened room. As soon as they had gone I seized a shard of mirror that still clung to the wall and drew it across my neck. Though I pressed the glass deep into my flesh the blood would not spill. I sliced into my wrists but left only dry gashes. And this horror, that I could not die, was truly greater than the horror of suicide.

"I left then, my house and my city, walking out past the shack where my love had lived, past his legacy of weeds and orchids. I walked out into the fields behind the city and on into the hills where the restless winds roam and I walked past those hills into the desert and here in these barren wastes I have been wandering many years searching for the doorway to the valleys of death. I am always thirsty, always hungry. I cannot die."

She fell silent and stared out at the dark sands. She did not weep. And Pico, though her story moved him more than any other heard on this journey, was too shocked to let tears come. He stared at her, gently stroked her hand, the hand that had touched for an instant a petal from the country of death, and she stirred a little.

"I cannot help you," he said. "I do not know where the threshold to the dry land might be."

"No," she shook her head. "You cannot tell me and perhaps it does not exist, that place where one may walk from this world to the next and return, but if I have no hope I have nothing. I hold my love for him before me like a flame to light my way in the darkness. But sir, you have helped me, you have drawn me water from the well and heard my story. I will not thirst this night, and my loneliness is eased."

She stood.

"Are you leaving?"

She smiled sadly. "The world is immense and I have traversed only a small portion of it. I must continue my search. I will not rest until I have found the doorway to death where my lover waits for me. I wish you luck in your own quest, young poet, but now I must leave you. Farewell."

He raised a hand but was unable to speak, watching her walk away from the well into the desert, and then he stood and took up his knapsack and set off himself, on a path at a right angle to hers. But though each step put a greater distance between them, they traveled the same road, for no direction, no quarter of the compass rose, is barren of the paths that lead to love.

He walked into the land of thirst. The sun fell in torrents, a storm of heat. He passed the noon hours with his head and shoulders in the wedge of shadow made by draping the blanket over his knapsack and battening the corners with sand. Too hot to sleep, though dreams came nonetheless, hallucinations he mumbled at. They went away. He rose and drank sparingly, then moved on into the rising night.

He made the water last two days, eking it out drop by drop. Then it was gone. On the morning of the third day he sat beneath the brute glower of the sun and held the bottle above his mouth. One drop hung. It fell. He tasted nothing. He corked the canteen, placed it in his pack and walked on.

Days passed. Two, three. Or perhaps only one. A day and a night, all eternity. Time had contracted to a single word: water. He could not turn back, he would die before he reached the well. He had come too far. He no longer knew why he moved. Why after he woke in the bitter dawn he stood and lifted the knapsack and stumbled on. Thirst had usurped all other thought. What would he sell now for a cupful of water? What use are dreams, poems, stories in the desert?

He fell to his knees, got up, fell again. He took off the knapsack and emptied the contents onto the sand. Spare clothes, tin pot, candles, groundsheet, twine. His blue velvet coat. He left them where they lay. Into the pack he placed again the folded blanket, the books from the city in the mountains, his notebook and fountain pen and empty water bottle. He walked on.

His lips were huge and gashed and when he touched them his fingers came away red. His tongue a foot shoved into his mouth, his eyelids pumice. Once he found himself facedown in the sand and could not recall having fallen. The sky swirled like stirred egg white. He discarded the blanket and books and knapsack then, and gripping the notebook, water bottle at his hip, floundered on.

Then he was crawling, clutching at handholds of sand, dragging himself forward. The sky was a vortex and the horizon flaked upward as though the earth were disintegrating, sucked into the hot maw above. The water bottle hindered his movement so he cast it aside. Much later, with a reluctance that seemed infantile when he tried to examine it, he dropped the notebook. He moved an arm. He moved a leg. He rested his head on the sand. He moved an arm. He moved a leg. And the sun, merciful mallet, beat him senseless.

Nine

The Morning Town

A shivering shade. The word ten thousand times silently repeated at last spoken onto his lips. When he tries to open his eyes he sees only thrashing fronds of gold. A noise like a bonfire about his ears, a tempest in his face. The sand gapes and he falls through a quaking shaft. Water on his lips and wind in his hair.

He wakes in a gray room, naked, in cool vaults of shadow, and peace lies upon his body like a quilt of water. There is a jug beside his pallet and he lifts it to his lips and drinks, then looks about him. A room of gray stone with a huge arch for a window, a curved gateway to nothing at all, blind eyeball, still pool, dreamless sleep.

Then a handful of gold dust is tossed into the abyss, and his heart is all at once a bird. Shedding weariness, he rises and moves to the window, sits within its curve and watches the winged people lift into a dawn sky, soaring above toppled towers and ruined statues to greet the sun.

What other arrival has he known, the sad poet? All his life has been a yearning but here at last a mission has come to completion. His journey is not over but it has entered a new room, he sits at the brink of beginning. Tears pry at the forms he watches, spindling them. He'd forgotten the bliss of watching the winged and feels again the tug in his shoulder blades, the old ache of his denied birthright.

Like pollen they rise, like dragonflies, scraps of foil, winking eyes, and he watches them swirl up through the lingering night which is the world's shadow and burst abrupt and brilliant into the high day. He cannot take his eyes from them, from their flitting and flirting, the filaments of their choreography a rope woven of sand, a cord braided by the wind, phantom, evanescent.

Only when they begin to fall like autumn leaves does he look at the landscape below, at the stone fists and elbows thrusting through the sand, the peaks of a drowned city. Here an enormous stone head lies on its side, one eye staring at the horizon, the other smothered by a dune. There like a circle of stone park benches a buried turret nudges its crenellation into the air. Many towers still crest the dunes, a petrified forest of crumbling trunks. Fragments of glazed tile cling to some like scraps of gaudy bark, faded lapis and rose, bespeaking former splendor. Body parts lie about like the aftermath of a war of statues. Corroded torsos, massive wrists, bent knees. In one place a great finger points into the sky and he imagines how deep he would have to dig to reach the giant's feet.

With a susurration like grass in a breeze the winged people settle over the ruins, wings cupping the air on the approach then folding like the furling of a hundred gilt fans. One lights upon the great stone head like a beautiful insect perched on an enormous corpse. They stand a moment, faces turned to the sun, then rise again and come toward him and circle the tower. He hears the shuffle of agitated air, the changed timbre as they enter windows.

Like the intrusion of a sudden gale a winged man dips into the archway Pico sits in and he stands, heart in throat, to greet him. And though his parents had resembled this creature, though he'd once kissed a winged girl, he is nevertheless dazzled by this being, wings like sheaves of gold leaves, hair scorched by the sun, mauled by the wind. The body lean as a spear, taut as a harp string, the color of wheat. Eyes clear and steady as the flame of a lantern. Though he is naked he has none of the awkward gestures ordinary humans adopt confronted by a stranger. He does not touch his arms as Pico does or twine his fingers together or bite his lower lip but stands with feet apart and hands at his sides watching the shy poet.

"Good morning, good morning, sir," Pico stammers.

The man nods, once. He looks at the jug by the pallet. "You have drunk?"

"Yes, thank you very much."

"You feel stronger?"

"I'm still rather weak, I'm afraid."

"Food will come." He squats with his elbows resting on his knees, face turned into the light.

"Please," says Pico after a while. "What is your name?"

The winged man looks at him a moment, then smiles. "You are new. Names are forgotten here. This is Paunpuam, the morning town."

"I have come to get my wings."

"Yes."

"Did you also come here to get your wings?"

"Yes."

"Where is your home?"

The man stretches a hand to the horizon, signifying perhaps that he comes from that portion of the world, or from the sky, or that he does not know. Pico doesn't feel able to pry further. Instead he asks, "When will I learn to fly?"

"You will be taken to read the book."

"The Book of Flying."

The man nods. Though his answers are short he does not seem impolite or unhelpful, rather Pico feels that conversation is not usual in this place. His companion appears much accustomed to silence.

A boy flutters through the archway. He sets before Pico a wooden bowl of dates and oranges and almonds, then squats beside the man. Under their unwavering gaze he eats, finding it difficult to chew with his damaged lips but managing to swallow some of the soft dates and several orange segments. When he is done the boy takes up the bowl and they stand.

"Sleep," says the man, and they leap into the air, into the hot morning, wings spraying like solid light.

Late in the afternoon he wakes refreshed. He goes through the door in the inner wall of the room and finds himself in a vast stairwell that coils about the hollow core of the tower. The stairs lack a banister and hugging to the wall he spirals down the tower passing door after door through which he glimpses sky or wings. Finally he arrives at an archway that will let him out onto sand, though the stairwell continues its descent, a plummet into circular darkness.

He wanders through the ruined town. The tower he has exited is the tallest of the structures, receding in tiers to a single room at the top canopied by a stone dome, open to the winds. Arched casements perforate the edifice and in some crouch winged people like inhabitants of an outsized dovecot. He walks among the fragments of enormous sculptures, circles the stone head, touching the ear in whose crevices he could nap like a cat in the folds of a blanket. An eye as tall as himself. What does a stone see? Who carved these statues, how long ago? Had those ancient sculptors been winged? He wonders whether any person alive knows the history of this town slowly succumbing to the sands.

Behind the tower he spies green and in the cool of evening comes among groves of date palms and orange and pomegranate, pistachio and almond trees, the air beneath them fragrant with blossom. He walks through shadows where doves call and after a while hears the sound of falling water and comes upon a fountain issuing from the mouth of a serpent into a stone bowl, relic of the ancient town, tapping some underground source. He stands in the shadow of the trees watching the water, listening to the voice of the fountain that is also the voice of the sea.

Like a falling star a young winged girl drops into the clearing, landing on the lip of the bowl, petite toes curling into the water. Fluttering a little to keep her balance, she turns her arms in the pour and lets the water break upon her face, enter her mouth. She combs it into her hair with her fingers. Dipping each foot into the basin, she splashes water up her legs, then, trailing a trickle of laughter, returns to the sky. She has not noticed Pico at all and he feels like an eavesdropper on some arcane ritual, though what could be more ordinary than a girl rinsing feet and arms at a basin.

He walks back through the fallen fruit and the arrows of sunset and as he emerges from the trees sees the great tower before him, luminous in the late light. Then it explodes. From the black orifices burst the winged people. Up and out they waft, ethereal, delirious, spiraling into a lake of honey. Higher, higher, and Pico's heart aches to be rid of his earthbound ribs, he raises his hands to the citizens of the air, his gods, then pulls his palms down over drenched cheeks.

In the morning town the winged people fly at dawn and dusk, they leave the rooms of the tallest tower through windows that are walls of sky and drift deep into the air, into the sky which constantly changes its attire, constantly shifts the winds which are its names. They seldom speak, the winged, and eat less. The sky sustains and nourishes them, they feed on the winds, on the light. They sleep in the afternoons and in the nights, crouched like marvelous eagles at the ledges where their chambers become sky, heads under wings, and their dreams are all of flying. Sometimes in the midst of these dreams a night breeze will tickle their feathers and they'll spread their wings and drift, dreaming still, out over the desert. They may wake alone under the stars and see the ruined town far below, burned bones strewn on linen sands, and will sink, circling, back to their chambers to continue the dreams anchored to stone. Under the ministry of moonlight the spare order of the desert sleeps.

In a room of winds at the top of the tower, a room circled by pillars and surmounted by a dome, a book lies in a box. A box carven from a single block of black stone, its lid scoured by eons of blown sand.

Early one morning Pico is shown to the room by a silent winged man who leads him up the stairs and through a circle in the floor and points to the box then leaps out into the sky. Pico sits cross-legged on the floor before the box and lifts the lid. The book within is large but not thick. He withdraws it from the stone coffer and runs his fingers across the cover, which is of ebony inlaid with designs in ivory and gold wire, the title traced in sapphires and blue beryls: THE BOOK OF FLYING.

He turns to the first page and instantly the tower and the sky, the desert and his very breath, his very heartbeat are snatched away and he is inside the book, the Book of Flying, the most beautiful book he has ever read.

All that day he reads, if reading is the word to describe the annihilation of his being that book induces. He will not remember turning the heavy vellum, will not remember the serpentining capitals colored like the wings of beetles or the full-page illustrations intricate as cities or the smaller sketches that sparkle in the interstices. He will not recall the careful strokes of each letter, the look of the ink on the skin, the edges where the pages are worn through by the caresses of countless thumbs. At the end of that day when at last he closes the back cover he is some minutes remembering his name for he has been absent from his body, wandering, a bare spirit, in the green meadows of the story he's desired all his life.

Buried within the books he'd read, the books of his library by the sea and the books of the city in the mountains, evident in a striking metaphor, a surge of passion within a paragraph, or simply an apt pairing of words, and caught also within certain larger motions of the stories, were the touchstones of his longing. He recognizes them now as those passages that came closest to the Book of Flying. All his life he has read like a man who embarks on a voyage with no destination in mind, or perhaps like a pilgrim who begins a journey to a distant shrine but, distracted by strange lands and marvelous characters, arrives elsewhere and has forgotten why he set off. Pico knows all his reading and writing have thrust him toward this book, and will forever be transformed by its memory. And he knows as well that he will never read it again, one cannot relive a moment of life save in memory, save in dreams.

But what is the book about? you clamor. Tell us the story, show us those marvelous illustrations. Oh I could say it is about a thief, a sword, a dream, a whore, and wings of course, wings, and it is, but what's the use? A fragment would tell you nothing for fragments of that book are in all books. The Book of Flying may be read only once, from beginning to end, at the far side of a journey undertaken for love,

on which death is tasted. You will read it or you will not. And though
you say you have not read it yet you know it. Look. Look deeper.

That night he wanders dazed among the ruins. He does not know
where he is, the book still within him vaster than the sand he treads,
more solid than the stone walls he touches. What he knows is that
some massive restlessness has woken in his chest, a dozing dragon,
which previously has only twitched in its sleep. Now it stirs its coils,
gapes its jaws. A craving, an itching, like the throb of sexual desire.

At dawn he weeps when the winged spray from the tower, and falls
to the sand distraught that he is not among them, that he alone in this
forgotten town remains earthbound.

While he lies thus in an agony of the spirit a winged woman descends. She takes his hand and lifts him to his feet and leads him into
the tower. Not up, not to his sleeping chamber or the room of winds
but down into the dark well, the shaft that augurs the earth.

Down they walk while the spark of light from the highest room
fades. Blind, questing for each step, a hand on the perimeter wall. The
echos of his breathing like moths in his ears. Down they spiral,
deeper, and he imagines this well has no ending, that they descend to
the center of the world, and indeed the air grows warm as if they near
the fires at the earth's heart.

At last beyond the thought of light they reach the end of that
stairway and the winged woman guides him through a doorway into a
chamber little wider than his arm span and there she removes his

clothes and lays him on the stone and he feels her hand across his eyelids, closing them.

"Sleep," she says and then is gone, the tempest of her wings diminishing in the shaft. Silence.

To fly one must believe and true belief can only occur in dreams.

Beneath a desert, buried in a chamber warmed by the hidden fires of the earth, Pico slumbers swaddled in sorrow. Blood pools in his shoulder blades. From all these dreams, a planet, solar system, universe of dreams, from the infinite intangible, arrives at last into the air a handful of feathers, the frugal reward for a lifetime of longing, a lifetime lived in the womb of the imagination.

Next to the hot pulse of the earth's heart he sleeps, he forgets, he grows wings.

In a long dawning into darkness he wakes, the winged man, flexes a hand, a foot, flexes the new muscles at his shoulders and hears the sweep of feathers along stone. The dream has entered the world and there will be no more sleep for he is at last alive. He rises and leaves the chamber where his memories and his name lie like a sloughed chrysalis, and he paces the steps into the darkness above. Up he walks, blind, feeling the new weight of the wings on his back, beautiful burden, and he emerges through a circle in stone into a room of night winds.

"How do you learn to fly?" He had asked the question of Sisi so long ago, in a forgotten conversation, and she had replied, "You fall."

The wings and the wind are his teachers. He leaps over the precipice.

When the winged people lift from the tower at dawn he is above them, turning in the still, bright air. Over the morning town of Paunpuam the newest airman rises to the sun.

Nameless he flies, drinks at the fountain, sleeps. There is no more memory, only the wind under his wings, the air in his lungs, the sun in his eyes. His body hardens, skin shifts its color to deep gold, dyed in an excess of light. When he dreams he dreams of flight. There is no conversation in the morning town. No other traveler arrives. Sometimes he lights in the branches of a date palm, an orange tree, and eats of the fruit but finds he is less and less hungry. His body is become light, a leaf, a leaf of light on the wind.

At dawn and dusk he flies, and in the afternoons and in the nights he sleeps at the edge of a wall of sky and sometimes he wakes from a dream of flying and finds he is turning in the cool air above the ruined tower. And on all sides, endless, the sands spill away from this center, from this haven of flight. There is no edge to the desert. He rises to greet the sun, bid it farewell, in an ecstasy of forgetting.

One morning at dawn he circles on the outer ring of the helix of winged people, flung far over the sands like a wasp on an invisible tether, and he spies below a shape that echoes. Perhaps it is rock, a stray morsel of some ancient turret, but without knowing why, he must investigate. He drops to the sand, kneels, tugs at the umber wedge that is not stone, that has nearly been concealed beneath the slow desert tides, pulls it free, turns the book in his hands. The gilt edges of the pages have been all but scoured away. He opens the book to the first page and there in the middle of the desert reads a poem and realizes only after he has finished that it is his own, that he has read a poem written years before in honor of a winged girl in a distant city by the sea.

He thinks he will drown as the memories flood back, he cannot breathe, the lock is breached and his lungs are filled to bursting. But memories are seldom fatal.

He carries his notebook back to the tower and that day reads it through, learning to know himself. And what he reads is strange and beautiful and he thinks it is more beautiful than his life of flight in the morning town, because it is sad.

He remembers Sisi, the arc of her laughter over him, her obsession with the sky, and all at once the love that had brought him to this place is uncovered within him, as a cloth may be swept off a lamp, as night turns to day. The love that has given him wings. And he realizes her kiss is worth more than his wings, worth more than a lifetime of flight. This act of remembrance is holy.

Ten

The Sea

That very night he sets off, lifting from the tower while the others sleep, carrying his notebook and his memories westward over the desert.

Flying is so swift. Before midnight he reaches the well where he had met Aia but lacking a pail he cannot drink and so flies on, shadow skimming in minutes spaces that had cost him hours of agony and by morning the desert is behind him, he has arrived at the foothills, the mountains rumpled drapes above him. There he drinks from a brook and sleeps in the lacy shade of an acacia and by midafternoon is lifting on a thermal over the dry shrubs, wheeling higher past the rutted skin of the mountains into freezing air, beating his wings now to keep the blood moving, until he is high enough to skim across the pass, over the vacant towers of the dark castle. He glimpses the courtyard solid white under new snow, then banks down on warmer breezes over the city in the mountains where spring has netted the chestnut trees in tender green. His shadow brushes the boulevard and he sees the waiters and strollers gape and call but he is gone, winging over slate roofs, over fields weighed down by floodwaters, and then he is over the forest. The leaves that had broken and shuttered the sun, the branches and trunks that had formed the corridors of a maze for him, are now a carpet of emerald and other greens, a green sea flowing beneath his wingbeats.

He sleeps the second night by the waterfall and in the morning rinses himself in its frigid smash, shakes out his feathers to dry.

Next day he flies over Master Rabbit's den and that night he sleeps in the forest. The next, the fourth since he started out from the morning town, he sleeps in Balquo's empty tower, between sheets he'd straightened himself how many months ago.

All the next day he flies, and well into the night, passing in the darkness fires that might belong to bands of robbers or other travelers beginning their own journeys, and he arrives in the early hours of the morning at the edge of the forest above the sea. There he sits, wings folded, the scent of the sea in his nostrils, waiting for dawn, waiting for the bells to peal in the hundred towers to send the winged people soaring on the wind, his love among them.

He is happy for this time of quiet alone at the end of his journey, while faces and voices drift like constellations through his memory. How full he is. Remembering the scant lad who'd left this hillside over a year ago, he laughs, touches the book, the notebook that holds those memories, and he silently salutes the earlier inhabitant of this body, that frail librarian who yet had the courage to jettison all and set off into dangerous and unknown territory in pursuit of a rainbow. Certain corners sparkle with images, the nameless lord of the dark castle had said, and maybe this is one, this boundary to the forest, adjacent to the sea and sky. Maybe unbeknown to him his former self indeed sits near him in the dark, awed by his wings.

Now the first birdsong crackles into the hush and he sees the sun has flung its first tresses forward into the night like a girl casting her damp hair over a balcony to dry. With the edges of his eyes he can divide the sea from the sky. The hills to left and right block swathes of sky and below him the rooftops appear dimly, but with an emotion like panic he sees that the silhouette of the town has changed. In his absence it has altered and he stands up, hands at his throat, choking on his heart, while the dawn brings into slow focus the diminished structures below him. No longer do the myriad towers spring jagged and lovely into the air, the towers with their bright tiles and arches and bells and doves and wings. Now only the low roofs of houses spread like tilled land before the sea. For a moment he thinks he's arrived at the wrong city but he turns and sees his library on the hill to his left, the statues stretching into the quiet air. The quiet air. Dawn in this city had always been loud with bells and the sound of wings. Now the light settles across silent streets.

Filled with bewilderment, not yet lamenting for he does not know the size of his loss, he walks to the library. The door is locked but the shutters of the cupola stand open and he flies softly up and lights on the windowsill where he once sat writing poems and looks into the room where Narya lies asleep upon the mattress, a dozen cats strewn about her. He steps into the room and kneels beside her and she opens her eyes. Still in the dreamy state where any sudden shift in surroundings is acceptable, she smiles. "Pico, you've come home."

She sits up, cats groaning and arching around her, and reaches a hand to his face, his wings, and laughs. "Pico. I can't believe it. You're so beautiful I hardly recognize you. Your wings. You have wings. You found the morning town."

He nods.

"Now you can fly."

He nods again. "Narya," he says, his voice like a run of sand in a bottle. "Narya. The towers."

She looks at him. "Come," she says. "I'll make some coffee."

They go down the spiral staircase into the library and he gasps and then begins to cry. The books and the shelves they had stood upon are gone. The walls are fresh white but the ceiling that had been filled with frescoes now bears rags and curtains of soot, in some places the underlying forms still showing through. A spray of feathers here, an eye there. Shadowed menagerie. The pieced marble of the floor is crazed and many tiles are replaced with shards that do not fit the pattern.

Narya puts her arm around him, holding him as he had held her, months before, or was it years? How long had he spent in the morning town? He realizes he has no idea. Those days had passed as one, days in the sun, the enchanted life of the winged. But now he stands in a burned room.

Narya opens the copper doors and in the gush of light he sees against one wall a single low shelf on which three books stand. He goes to them, kneels beside them. They are the books he had chosen for his journey, the book of poems, the book of stories, the novel, that he had later given to Narya. In taking them he had unwittingly rescued them and now they are the sole books in the library, perhaps in the entire city.

"The fire," he says.

She nods. "I arrived here soon after the city burned. People were scouring the rubble of the destroyed towers for valuables. I saw some of the bells, melted into meteorites. I gathered fragments of the roofs to replace the tiles here." She splays a hand to the floor.

"And the winged people?" he whispers.

"Gone." She turns to look out the bright doorway, then swivels back to him, touching his wings shyly. "You are the first winged person I have seen."

"Gone where?"

"There are other stories to tell first."

The irises still grow outside the door, a bed of torn purple tissue paper on which secrets are scribbled. He picks a bloom and sits on a step clutching it to his chest while she lights a small stove and fills a pot at the well and sets it on the fire. She joins him on the step and rolls a cigarette and holds it out but he shakes his head so she smokes alone.

"Tell me about your journey," he says, so while they drink the coffee, while the sun rises and the city folk move into the streets and the laughter of children bubbles up like spindrift and the fishing boats set off upon the water, he hears her story, with its own inventory of queer characters, marvelous conversations, terrors, reprieves. It is nearly noon when she finishes.

"How strange," he says. "I had imagined your story would be mine reversed, the same events encountered in the opposite direction, but each person's journey, I suppose, is new."

"And," she says, "you must remember that your passage through the world has altered it irrevocably. Certain houses stand empty because of your passage, people you met have set off on journeys of their own, as I did. The forest you entered is not the one you left behind."

"Even memory changes the world. A voice, a face, may only be encountered once."

"Now it's your turn. What did you find in the dark castle?"

So he tells her of the lonely sculptor who bore his own face and the release of the city from its long torment and she shudders when he tells how Solya's flesh had sustained him, then nods. "Solya once said all food has been human flesh and will return to flesh again. She would have been delighted to be eaten by you, I believe."

He tells of the journey into the desert, of his arrival at the well. She shivers again when he relates Aia's tale. He tells of the dry land, the land of stones, of how he thought he would die there, and of his rescue by the winged people. Finally he tells what he remembers of the morning town and the Book of Flying, though it seems a dream, more distant than his time in the city in the mountains, more distant even than his years in the library.

"Do you remember, Narya, telling me that we are all searching for some pristine story? One night, late, we were in my garret room, the snow was falling."

"The story we all remember but never find."

"I found the story, Narya. The Book of Flying."

"Your story."

"Yes."

"But just as each journey is unique, each story is unique. I have no wish for wings. The story I seek is another story. Perhaps it will arrive here from across the sea."

They sit in silence awhile looking out across the water. They hear the voices of children playing on the outskirts of the city.

"Now," he says.

"It was soon after I arrived," she begins, then puts her face in her hands. "Oh Pico, I can't tell you this story," and all at once he is calm. "Tell me, Narya," he says. "It is my story. I must accept it."

"Oh, I wish it had not come to me to tell it."

"Narya." He takes her hand.

She sighs. "Soon after I arrived here, after I had swept out the debris, the charred wood and scraps of blackened paper, I had a visitor. I had taken a break from painting the walls and was sitting on this step smoking when a small boy came up the hill. He held in his hand a rolled piece of paper tied with yellow cord and when he reached me he handed me the paper and asked if it spoke. He said that his mother told him that the paper could speak, that he should come to the library to find out what it said. I untied the knot and saw that it was not an ordinary scrap of paper but the finest parchment and on the parchment was written in purple ink a fragment of a poem. I invited the child to join me on the steps and read the poem aloud to him and then I asked the child where he'd found it. He told me this story.

"Before the burning, when the tall houses were still here, he said, before all the blood, before the winged people flew away, he woke one morning and thought it was a festival because everyone was singing and shouting in the street. His house was empty so he went out as well, into the street. A coffin was being carried through the city and his family and neighbors and everyone else were gathered around it shouting and singing and crying, this is what the little boy told me.

"In the coffin a winged girl lay, the prettiest one, he said, and at first he thought she was sleeping but his mother told him she was dead. She had paper all around her, some pieces rolled and tied with ribbons, some she held in her dead hands. He said she was still pretty even though she was dead.

"'How did she die?' he asked his mother and she said the girl had fallen into the sea. Had someone pushed her? he asked but his mother said that no, she had wanted to go into the sea because she was tired of flying.

"He followed the coffin through the streets because of the singing and because the winged girl was so pretty. As the procession came out onto the hill where the graveyard was, the wind blew some of the pieces of paper into the air and he chased one and caught it. He thought it was a treasure so he kept it in his room to remember the winged girl. His mother had found it when she was cleaning his room and told him it could speak.

"I asked the boy the name of the dead girl but he didn't know. The prettiest one, he said again."

"Do you remember the poem?" Pico asks.

She recites several lines then turns to him but he does not look at her. He stands and goes into the library and climbs the stairs to the cupola and fetches the notebook which he had left on the windowsill. The notebook he had begun to write in after Sisi had left him, that he had carried through a forest and across mountains, over a desert, that had been discarded and found, had taught him his name when he had forgotten it and allowed him to leave the morning town. He carries the notebook down to Narya and sits beside her and opens it to a page near the beginning. She bends over the scrawl then looks up, eyes awash.

"Pico. Oh Pico."

But he does not cry, not then. He takes her tears onto his fingers and looks at them. The sun makes rainbows inside the droplets.

"What will you do, Pico?" she sobs.

"Here." He hands her the notebook. "For the library. You had three books, now you have four. This is how libraries are built, book by book, until they are burned again. Other books will arrive from across the sea for this is not the first burning. The library has burned before, it will burn again and be rebuilt. Book by book.

"But Narya, this place has become dangerous for me. I left the library to find wings that I might be accepted in my city, that I might find love here, but instead I have exiled myself from it. They will kill me if they find me."

"Yes."

"I must leave at once. Some children may already have seen me and run to tell their parents. Soon they will come looking for the winged man. Though I am weary my journey is far from over. Perhaps it has only just begun."

She looks sadly at him.

"But I was happy to find you here." Pico touches her cheek. "A face I knew, a voice that knew my name."

"I will hold your name in my heart."

"We have kissed before. Kiss me now, for you will never see me again."

Her kiss tastes of salt and iron for she has bitten her lip in her grief. She strokes his wings.

"Go," she says.

So the sad poet, winged now, lifts over the city, the white city in the sun by the sea, like a great gull, like the ghost of the sun itself. Once he circles, leaving a wake of cries below, cries of anger and cries of wonder as well, and then sweeps out over the sand and across the waves. He skims over the sea weeping, the last winged man, salt water falling to salt water. And though he tries to flee his tears, the sea itself is all the tears of those who've ever wept. Even the sea, even the sundering sea will not set the sad poet apart, for the country of sorrows is the size of the heart.